AUTUMN BLEEDS INTO WINTER

JEFF STRAND

AUTUMN BLEEDS INTO WINTER

JEFF STRAND

1

In the summer of 1979, a few days after my fourteenth birthday, I was in the back of a van with an airbrushed panther on the side, trying to buy an untraceable pistol.

I lived in Fairbanks, Alaska. The kind of safe neighborhood where kids would be turned loose in the morning and left to their own devices until the piercing shout of their mother informed them that it was time to come home for dinner. The neighborhood dogs just walked wherever they wanted, unleashed, and we knew each of them by name.

Oh, sure, we had bullies, but not the kind that left lasting trauma. Throughout the second grade, my friends and I lived in fear of a kid we'd nicknamed Checkers because he always wore a red-and-black checkered jacket. He was a huge, scary-looking kid— a third-grader for sure. If we saw him on the playground during recess, and he saw that we saw him, he'd immediately give chase and we'd flee in terror. Sometimes we'd lose him quickly, and sometimes we'd spend the entirety of recess trying to escape a savage beating that would presumably involve broken bones and spurting blood.

The only thing saving us was that his frightening bulk was perfect for intimidation but not so great for endurance in a pursuit.

The playground had some gigantic tires stacked on top of each other. You could climb on the outside of them or also crawl around inside the tires themselves. (I honestly don't know if they were somehow attached or, by 1970's playground safety standards, just stacked with the assumption that they probably wouldn't come crashing down and kill several children.) One day, I was inside the highest tire and when I glanced down, there was Checkers, looking up at me. I was trapped. There was no escape. I was filled with the white-hot terror of a second grader who knows that a bloody nose is in his future.

"I've got you now!" said Checkers. Then he let out a maniacal, villainous laugh.

And I suddenly realized that he meant me no harm. While my friends and I were completely convinced of the peril we faced from Checkers, he was just having fun chasing some younger kids around the playground. He never caught us because he didn't want to. If he *had* caught us, he would've simply released us, like fish.

As I got older, there were other bullies, the kind who might try to trip you in the cafeteria or hurl epithets that were much more acceptable a few decades ago than they are today. But there really wasn't much in the way of danger. There were rumors that a kid froze to death when he forgot his house key and his parents were late getting home from work, but I didn't know him and the story didn't really hold up to close scrutiny. Overall, it was a very safe childhood.

Until some kids disappeared.

And I knew exactly who did it.

I knocked on the side door of the van, which was parked at our designated meeting spot in front of The Old House. The house probably wasn't older than any other house in the neighborhood, but it had been abandoned for as long as I could remember, and it was falling apart to the extent that even kids who thought they were protected by the invincibility of youth didn't venture inside. But with the overgrown yard, you could park a van in front of it and not attract any real attention.

The door slid open. A man with greasy long hair and a thick mustache looked surprised to see me.

"Fuck off, kid," he said. "I'm meeting somebody."

"You're meeting me."

"The hell I am."

"I'm Curtis."

The man groaned. "Are you kidding me? What are you, nine?"

"I'm fourteen."

"Sorry, kid. I don't sell guns to chubby fourteen-year-olds. Go away."

"My money's as good as anybody else's."

The man massaged his forehead as if this decision was causing him intense pain. "Fine, fine, whatever. Get in."

I climbed into the van, which smelled like what I was innocent enough to believe was a dead skunk. I started to pull the door closed.

"Don't close it all the way," he told me. "I don't want you to be able to say I tried to kidnap you."

I closed the door most of the way. The inside of the van had a mattress on the floor and red blankets. I was *not* so innocent as to think, "Oh, this must be in case he wants to sleep in his van during road trips!"

He lit a normal cigarette and glared at me. "This isn't cool at all."

"Sorry."

"What do you want a gun for, anyway? You're not going to shoot your teachers, are you?"

"No."

"Don't your parents own a gun?"

"Sure they do. A bunch of them." This was Alaska. Every household had a gun collection.

"So why don't you use one of those?"

"Because I don't want it to be traceable. That's the whole reason I called you. If I wanted something for target practice, I'd ask my dad to let me borrow a rifle."

"Why don't you want it to be traceable?"

"Why are you asking so many questions?"

"Because I don't sell guns to kids. I don't know what you're going to do with it. What if you're dumb? What if you accidentally blow your face off? I don't want that coming back on me."

"The whole point is that the gun can't be traced. If it comes back on you, then you're bad at your job."

"It's not my job. It's just a side gig."

"Are you going to sell me a gun or not?"

The man took a drag from his cigarette and blew the smoke in my face. "Are you planning to kill somebody with it?"

"None of your business," I told him, trying not to cough. If I coughed, he'd have the upper hand in our little power struggle.

"You sure as hell aren't planning to use it to shoot squirrels, so you're either going to commit a murder, or you're going to plant it on somebody to get them in trouble. Which is it?"

"How do you know it's not just for self-defense?"

"Then why would it need to be untraceable?"

I honestly didn't know who was winning the argument. "I can't force you to sell me one. I'll just take my business someplace else."

"Good. Get out of my van."

I reached for the door handle, hoping he would suddenly change his mind. He said nothing.

I really didn't have another option. Finding this guy had been extremely difficult. The Internet didn't exist back then, and in fact if somebody had described the wonders of the World Wide Web as something that would be available in my lifetime, I would've gaped at them in slack-jawed astonishment, and then laughed in their face for believing something so ridiculous.

I figured that a drug dealer would know how to get a gun. I didn't know any drug dealers. I did, however, know a couple of older kids who I was relatively certain liked to smoke weed. (I didn't know what marijuana smelled like, but I knew what it was. Those educational films we watched in class weren't a complete waste.)

I paid them five bucks to give me the phone number of their dealer. I called him and asked if he knew how I could get an untraceable gun. He hung up on me. I called back later and a different person answered. I asked the same question, and while he didn't know, he gave me the phone number of another pot dealer who might. I called that dealer, and he said that he had no idea and wouldn't tell me even if he did.

So I called the other dealer back, and this time the first guy answered, and I apologized for bothering him and asked if he could sell me some marijuana (though, to make sure he didn't suspect I was a fourteen-year-old with no marijuana experience, I called it "Mary Jane") and also recommend a prostitute. He said to call him back in half an hour about the Mary Jane (I didn't) but gave me the number of an affordable hooker. I called Candi-with-an-I and asked if she knew anybody who could sell me a gun, and she passed me on to Barbarella, who gave me the number of this guy in the van whose name I didn't know.

It's worth noting that I was so committed to acquiring this firearm that I barely thought about the fact that I'd spoken to two prostitutes, and my own sexual experience maxed out at one astoundingly inept makeout session in a dark closet at a birthday party.

The man didn't try to stop me from leaving his van without purchasing an illegal weapon.

"I know who abducted the kids," I said.

"What kids?"

"You haven't heard about the missing kids?"

"Should I have?"

"It's on the news."

"I don't watch the news. And I don't like kids. For example, you're a kid, and I don't like you."

I hated to blab my plan to a stranger, but it didn't seem like he was going to budge otherwise. "I know who's doing it, but I can't prove it. I'm going to make him confess."

"At gunpoint? That won't hold up. People will confess to anything at gunpoint. You point a gun at me and I'll tell you anything you want to hear. I'll tell you I'm a Kenny Rogers fan."

"You don't like Kenny Rogers?"

"Nope. I'll whack off to Dolly Parton, but I hate that country music shit."

"I'm not going to make him confess at gunpoint," I said. "I'm just going to make him confess. But if he tries to kill me, I'm going to kill him first. If I have to shoot him before I have proof, I don't want anybody to trace it back to me. That's why I can't use one of my dad's guns."

The man nodded. "That makes sense. But it would be irresponsible for me to sell you a gun, knowing that you might kill an innocent man."

"He's not innocent."

"You said you don't have proof."

"I have my own eyes. Being able to prove it isn't the same as being positive."

"You know what? Screw it. I'll sell you a gun. There's gonna be a surcharge, though."

"What kind of surcharge?"

"The 'chubby fourteen-year-old' surcharge. It's a new thing."

"No. You said you'd sell me an untraceable pistol for three hundred."

"And now it's four hundred. That's how the free market works. You'll learn that someday when you get out of elementary school."

"I brought the amount we agreed to over the phone."

"Yeah, well, over the phone you messed with your voice to make yourself sound older."

He had me there. I'd put a cloth over the mouthpiece.

"I only have three hundred dollars."

"Then run on home and crack open your piggy bank, or ask your mommy for an advance on your allowance. Tell her the ice cream man raised his prices."

"You're an asshole," I told him.

"Well, yeah, I could've told you that. Now are you going to make me wash out your mouth with soap?"

"I guess we're done, then. You're lucky I can't contact the Better Business Bureau."

"You know what? Three-fifty."

"I literally only brought three hundred dollars. You know why? Because on the phone you told me the price was three hundred dollars. I assumed that old people like you kept their word."

"Where'd you get that much money, anyway?"

"I mowed a lot of lawns," I told him. I was lying. I'd taken the money from my dad's safe. Yes, I was the kind of kid who snooped through his father's desk and found the safe combination. There was quite a bit of money in there, because Dad didn't trust banks very much and wanted to have cash on hand in case of an emergency. I doubted he ever pulled the stacks of bills out of there to count them, so my plan was to gradually replace what I'd taken before he noticed it was missing.

"You got anything else valuable on you?" he asked. "What about that watch?"

"It's a cheap scratched-up watch."

"Oh, yeah. That's a piece of crap. Nobody would buy that. What about your shoes?"

"Then I'd have to make up a story to my parents about how I lost my shoes. I'm too old to just lose a pair of shoes."

"Fine. Three hundred dollars. The only reason I'm doing this is so I didn't drive all the way out here for nothing. But do you see the way I'm looking at you right now? What I'm doing is memorizing your face. So if I find out that an innocent person got shot, I'll be able to describe you to the sketch artist."

I was confident that he wouldn't go to the police and tell them he'd sold an illegal firearm to a fourteen-year-old boy, but I didn't call him out on that because I wanted to move this transaction along. "That's fair," I said.

He reached under one of the pillows and took out a pistol. Then he reached under another pillow and took out a small box of ammunition.

"This gun looks kind of shitty," I said.

"It is shitty. You should have specified that you wanted a non-shitty gun when we spoke on the phone. It won't blow up in your hand and it'll fire a bullet at whatever you point it at."

"What kind of gun is it?" I asked.

"How the hell should I know? It's a gun with the serial number filed off. You want a scholarly dissertation, go to a licensed dealer. Now, you do know that the gun itself is untraceable, but that they can trace a bullet back to the gun, right? So if they dig the bullet out of the person you used it in self-defense against, and they find the gun under your bed, they can do some tests to say that the bullet was fired from that specific gun. What I'm saying is, get rid of it when you're done."

"I will. Thanks." I took the wad of bills out of my pocket and handed it to him.

He quickly flipped through the bills, counting them. "Okay, we're good. I honestly thought you were going to hand me a jar of pennies."

I unzipped my backpack and put the gun and ammunition inside. Then I slid the door all the way open.

"Hey, kid?"

"Yeah."

"Be careful. I mean that. You're a little jerk but I don't want you to get hurt."

"I'll be as careful as I possibly can," I said, getting out of the van.

As I walked away from The Old House, I suddenly felt sick to my stomach. This was one great big step closer to being real now. I might indeed have to kill the man who'd abducted my best friend.

2

Todd and I had been friends ever since he took a checkmark on my behalf.

The deal in Mrs. Starkling's fourth grade class was that if you got in trouble for something, she wrote your name on the upper right corner of the chalkboard. That was your first warning. Everything was still cool, but you'd been put on notice. If there was a second infraction (it didn't matter if it was a repeat of the first or a whole new variety of misbehavior) you got a checkmark next to your name. Now shit was getting real. There were no specific consequences to the first checkmark except the shame. But you were only one inappropriate giggle from the *second* checkmark. You needed to start thinking very seriously about your attitude and how you could improve it.

If you got the dreaded second checkmark, you were on your way to visit the principal, who waited with his paddle to administer corporal punishment. My understanding is that he went easier on the girls or the younger kids, but if you were a fourth grade boy, he beat your ass without mercy. And the parents were totally fine with it. To the best of my knowledge, there was no form they could fill out to say "*I withhold permission for you to beat my child's ass during school hours.*" If you came home crying...well, you should have behaved in class.

Nobody knew what would happen if you got a third checkmark. I assume that Mrs. Starkling would just club you in the back of the head with a sledgehammer and drag you off to the slaughterhouse. Every Friday before school let out, she'd erase the names, and announce to those of us who'd been naughty that we would start with a clean slate on Monday.

Now, I was not a *bad* kid. I studied hard, got decent grades, and tried to pay attention as much as possible. But I couldn't keep out of my own head, which caused me to come up with fascinating observations that had to be shared with the kids around me, immediately. This was, of course, "talking in class." I got a hell of a lot of checkmarks for talking in class.

Worse, I'd conjure up mental images of such side-splitting hilarity that even if I bit down on the sides of my mouth hard enough to draw blood, I couldn't keep from laughing. I'd imagine that Mrs. Starkling, while walking down my row, let loose with a thundering, extended trumpet solo of flatulence. "Oh, *dear,*" she'd say. The "Oh, *dear,*" is the part that always got me.

To be clear: there was no actual incident of flatulence. But thinking about the possibility of this happening ("Oh, *dear!*") was so uproariously hysterically screamingly funny that I could not keep silent. Mrs. Starkling would ask if I wanted to explain to the class what was so amusing. I would answer that, no, I did not wish to explain this. And my name would go up on the chalkboard, if it wasn't there already.

The truth was, I didn't fear a visit to the principal. I'd been there twice, and though it was not an experience that I cherished, the pain went away after I was no longer required to remain seated. What really hurt was the thought of missing out on Movie Day.

One fine Monday we were told that Friday would be Movie Day. We would do the usual learning until lunch, and then after lunch the lights would go out and we'd get to watch a non-educational motion picture! Oh my God! There'd even be—brace yourself—popcorn! But because Mrs. Starkling was allowed to change the rules at any time, there was a plot twist: if you got a checkmark, just one, you would *not* be part of the glory of Movie Day. You'd be sitting in a different classroom with the other wicked children, doing an assignment specifically crafted to be as boring as possible. Presumably somebody would walk up and down the rows with a bowl of popcorn, taunting you with its buttery scent.

I vowed that I would not miss Movie Day.

But..."Oh, *dear!*"

That was Monday. I got my name written on the board on Tuesday, but I made it through to Friday morning without a checkmark. Then I forgot myself and right in the middle of a math lesson I asked the kid next to me if he'd seen *Sanford & Son* that week.

Mrs. Starkling spun around. "Who was talking?" she demanded, looking straight at me. She knew perfectly well who'd been talking, but she was going to wring a confession out of me anyway.

I froze. What had I done? Oh, God, what had I done?

"It was me, I'm sorry," said Todd Lester.

Todd never got in trouble. Ever. He wasn't some smarmy little suck-up who sat in the front row and raised his hand first for every single question, but his behavior record was spotless. I knew him only as a fellow student in Mrs. Starkling's fourth grade class; we didn't play together at recess, and I didn't even know which bus he took home. There was absolutely no reason for him to take the rap for me, except to be a nice guy and keep a screwup like me from missing Movie Day.

He sat two rows away. He obviously wasn't the one who'd been talking. Mrs. Starkling looked at him, looked back at me, sighed, and then wrote Todd's name on the chalkboard. She returned to the lesson without further scolding.

I couldn't believe he'd done that for me.

Todd was a far more fascinating human being than I'd ever imagined.

Before lunch, I had an uncontrollable fit of giggles ("Oh, *dear!*") and forfeited my right to Movie Day, so he'd sacrificed his flawless reputation for nothing. But as I sat in the mostly empty classroom doing the bullshit assignment, I vowed that I'd pay him back for his act of kindness.

After school let out, I hurried over to Todd as he walked toward his bus. "How was the movie?" I asked. "No, don't tell me. I don't want to know. I'm sure it was great. Thanks for saving me."

He stopped walking. "Were you dropped on your head as a baby?"

"No."

"Are you sure? Should you ask your mom and dad about it?"

I explained why I couldn't stop giggling in class. He stared at me, not quite comprehending why *imaginary* flatulence would have such an impact on me. Real flatulence, sure, of course, everybody can enjoy that, but cracking up over fictional flatulence was very odd to him.

"But I wanted to thank you anyway," I said. "I owe you a Twinkie or something."

"Fine. I'd love a Twinkie. Hand it over."

"I don't have one with me. But we've got a box of them at home. I thought maybe you might want to come over."

"I can't ride your bus without a permission slip."

"We could walk."

"How far?'

"It's too far to walk. I don't know why I said that."

Todd stared at me like I was a complete idiot. He was right to do so.

I wasn't sure he was going to resume the conversation, so I continued it for us. "Sorry. I'm stupid. This is probably why we're not friends."

"We can walk to my house," he said. "It's not that far."

"Will your parents get worried if you're late?"

"They won't be home."

"Sure, I'd like to come over. Can I call my mom from your house?"

"Yeah."

"Then let's go!"

Todd and I walked to his house. As it turned out, we had very different definitions of "not that far." It would've been faster to walk to my house. I'd been starting to put on some weight, so walking more than an hour left me short of breath and requesting occasional rest breaks. One of those rest breaks was at a payphone, where I went further into Todd's debt by borrowing a dime so I could call home. I'd thought "not that far" meant twenty minutes, maximum.

Our conversation during the walk was not that of kids who felt like they'd been friends their entire lives. We talked about superficial fourth grader stuff. When we got to his house, I was extremely impressed by his comic book collection, so after a lecture on how to properly care for them—I was a "fold the front cover around the back for ease of reading" kind of guy—we read and had a detailed discussion about some exciting superhero adventures.

(In case you were horrified by that last sentence, I'd like to break from the narrative to explain that for much of human history the comic book was seen primarily as disposable reading material, rather than collecting material. So I wasn't some raging comic book-destroying psychopath; it was, in fact, standard operating procedure to fold the front cover around to the back. Cultures evolve and in contemporary society I would be shunned and perhaps put to death for such disrespectful treatment of a graphic novel, but back then, *Todd* was the weird one, not me.)

After that, we became very casual friends. He had his own small social group and I had my own even smaller one, and there was no real spillover between them. The school year ended and we didn't see much of each other over the summer. When fifth grade started, we were in the same class again, and in Christmas 1975, everything changed.

Todd got Pong.

Pong was the most astounding revolution in entertainment of its time. For those not in the know, when you hooked up the Pong device to your television, a small white square would move back and forth across the screen. You did not control this square. You did, however, use the controllers to move the dashes that were on each side. You would use these dashes to block the path of the square, bouncing it back in your opponent's direction, hoping that he or she would fuck up and fail to block its path, thus causing you to score a point. If this sounds like table tennis, that's exactly what it was, except that *you played it on your television set!*

Todd invited me over to play Pong and I never wanted to leave. We'd play for hours. Our friendship grew with each exchange of trash talk. When we eventually got bored with Pong (unthinkable, I know) we continued to hang out almost every weekend. Though we still had other friends, Todd was always the first person I called if I wanted to socialize. Sometimes our parents would drop us off at each other's houses, but if not, the bicycle ride was a hell of a lot faster than the walk.

When Todd's family moved to the subdivision next to mine, we became inseparable. Our overall social standing, which had been adequate in elementary school, began to decline in junior high, but we were mostly okay with it. We still went to the school dances, we just didn't, you know, *dance*. We talked about girls a lot, and Todd went on an actual date that led to a brief timeframe where he wasn't sure if he had an actual girlfriend or not. (When he finally asked, she informed him that, no, he did not.)

Hanging out together, I got into less trouble and he got into more trouble. It was a nice balance.

We finished seventh grade in May 1979. We talked excitedly about starting eighth grade in the fall, and I vowed to get in shape by then. I'd put on enough weight that gym class had become something to dread each day.

Most of the summer was great. I did not get in shape.

At the end of May, a kid went missing. A sixth-grader. We didn't know him. Todd and I lived out by the airport, and the kid lived on the other side of Fairbanks, up by Farmer's Loop. Apparently he was a troubled child, and though nobody was ruling out an abduction, he'd most likely run away from home. When his parents were on television, they begged their son to come back, rather than pleading to the abductor for his safe return. It wasn't the type of situation to make parents fear to let their children go out without adult supervision.

In early July, Todd and I had a fight.

It was not a huge fight. Nothing friendship-ending. The kind of fight we might not even bother to acknowledge the next day. I made a joke about his mother that didn't land properly, he got pissed, and he no longer wanted to spend the night. He decided to walk home. It was one in the morning.

In most places, a thirteen-year-old would not be allowed to walk home alone at one in the morning, even in 1979. I would've woken up my parents, or he would've called his own to pick him up. But this was Fairbanks, Alaska. Land of the midnight sun. In July, the darkest time of night was like dusk anywhere else. And I lived in a safe neighborhood.

He left.

A couple of minutes later, I went after him.

Oh, it wasn't to beg for forgiveness, or to make sure he made it home okay. I'm ashamed to admit that I was angry that he'd taken such great offense to my harmless joke about my desire to bang his mom, so my plan was to sneak ahead of him, jump out, and scare the crap out of him.

I brought my mouse mask. This was an unlicensed Mickey Mouse mask that looked less like the delightful Disney mascot and more like a nightmare plague rat that would gnaw off your lips while you slept. It had been a gift from my grandmother when I was eight, and I'd been too scared to wear it at Halloween. Once I'd gotten over my fear, around age eleven, the cheap plastic mask was taken out of the back of my closet and went to its new home on my floor.

I did not think that Todd would believe he was being attacked by Mickey Mouse's rabid cousin. But jumping out at him in a mask would be scarier than jumping out at him with my regular face.

My neighborhood was a grid that was eight streets divided by three other streets, creating twenty-four blocks. The grid was surrounded on three sides by woods. If you knew the path your angry best friend was taking home, you could hop on your bicycle, quickly ride to the street parallel to the one your friend was taking, get far ahead of him, ditch the bike right before sneaking into the woods, and await his approach.

I did this.

I waited.

He came around the corner, a couple of blocks away. I put on the mask.

I hoped that after I leapt out at him, he'd punch me in the arm, we'd laugh, and our friendship would immediately revert back to where it had been ten minutes ago.

A silver car drove slowly past me.

It stopped next to Todd.

I watched, wondering what the driver wanted. At least I knew that Todd wasn't stupid enough to get into a car with a stranger at one in the morning.

He walked over to the driver's side door, apparently talking to the driver through an open window but keeping a safe distance.

Todd put his hand to his mouth.

Burst into tears.

What the hell was going on? What had the driver said to him?

Todd hurried around the front of the vehicle.

Did he know the driver?

He wasn't...he wasn't really getting in, was he?

The door opened and Todd got into the passenger side. I ran out onto the street as the car drove off. It turned at the next corner. I tried to remember the license plate number.

Had the driver seen me in his rearview mirror?

It was weird to be praying that Todd bursting into tears was because he'd been given actual terrible news and not that he'd been duped. What if his parents had been in an accident? What if they were *dead*? That was nightmarish but still better than the thought that he'd been kidnapped.

Not bothering to take off the mask, I jumped onto my bicycle and rode as fast as I possibly could. I wasn't trying to catch up to the car, but if I pedaled like a madman and he didn't take the most efficient route out of the neighborhood, I might be able to make our paths cross again.

My front tire wobbled, but I kept myself from falling off the bike. Todd's life might depend on this.

I was already out of breath as I approached the street where I thought I might see the car again. I had no idea what I'd do if I reached it. I was so desperate to save my friend that I didn't even consider that I might be putting myself in serious danger.

I could hear the car. I needed to go faster.

I wasn't going to reach the street in time!

The car crossed the intersection. The driver's side was facing me, and I saw the man behind the wheel. He glanced over and looked right at me.

The car screeched to a halt.

I knew the driver.

Not his name, but I'd seen him outside a couple of times, doing yard work. He lived in Todd's subdivision, maybe seven or eight blocks away from him. He was pretty old, somewhere between my dad and my grandfather's age, and he had a thick head of gray hair. He had a hard, unfriendly appearance, making me feel like I was trespassing when I walked past his house even though I was on the sidewalk.

The man quickly looked away, probably forever traumatized by the sight of the terrifying mouse mask.

The car sped off.

3

I chased after the silver car, but didn't even come close to catching up.

I decided to ride my bicycle to Todd's house instead of going back and waking up my parents. Maybe the man was a family friend. Maybe he was driving Todd to the hospital right now. I knew *something* bad had happened to make Todd burst into tears, but hopefully it was a temporary problem—perhaps his dad had a heart attack scare that turned out to be a false alarm.

The silver car was not in Todd's driveway. His mom's car and his dad's car were both there, but that didn't mean they hadn't left in an ambulance.

I removed the mask and pounded on the door.

It took a couple of minutes for somebody to answer. Finally Todd's dad opened the door, wearing only briefs. His look of annoyance disappeared when he saw that it was me, replaced by sudden concern.

"Curtis, what's wrong?" he asked.

I told him everything. By the time I was finished, his mom had joined us at the front door. His dad worked with a couple of people who owned silver cars, but nobody who would have had any reason to deliver bad news to his son.

It felt like it took forever for the state trooper to arrive, though it was probably a completely reasonable timeframe. While we waited, I had tried and failed to remember the license plate, though I knew there was a B and a 7. Not enough to trace it, but if we found a car with a B and a 7 in the license plate, that should be enough to prove it was the same vehicle.

I quickly repeated the story, while the state trooper—who looked a lot like Christopher Reeve in *Superman: The Movie*, which I took as a good sign—nodded and jotted down notes. He told Todd's parents to wait at home in case Todd called or came back home, and then I got into the front seat of the patrol car to show the state trooper where the man lived.

Or, where I *thought* he lived. I suddenly doubted my ability to take him straight to the correct house. I'd only seen the man a couple of times, and he hadn't made enough of an impression for me to recall important details like the color of his home. I could get us to the right street for sure. After that, I had to pray that I'd immediately recognize the place.

"Which house?" the state trooper asked.

None of them looked familiar. And I suddenly questioned whether Clerk Street was even the right street. All I'd ever done is walk past the man. We'd never even exchanged a friendly greeting. How was I supposed to remember where he lived?

There was a one-story tan house with a nice yard. That could be it.

"I think it's that one," I said, pointing.

"But you're not positive?"

"No."

He pulled up in front of the house. "I'm going to have you

scoot way down," he said. "There's no reason for anybody to know that you're the one who brought me here. Just in case you're wrong. Stay in the car until I get back."

I nodded and bent down underneath the window. The state trooper got out of the car.

Please let this be the right house.

Please let Todd be okay.

I hoped my parents hadn't noticed that I was gone. They might be worried. Although I supposed their first step would be to call Todd's house...which would be cruel to his parents, since they'd think the ringing phone would bring news about their son.

I was feeling dizzy and wanted to throw up.

I shouldn't have made that joke about his mom. This was all my fault.

A few minutes later, the door opened and the state trooper got back into the car. "It wasn't the right house," he told me. "But I described the man and they told me where he lives. You were close."

He drove three houses down. Yes, this was definitely the right place. I now remembered him, trimming some bushes, glaring at me as I walked past.

The state trooper told me to duck down again. I did.

I didn't pop my head up to look out the window, even when this seemed to be taking a long time. In the rearview mirror I saw another state trooper patrol car pull up in front of the house, and two more men got out.

Please don't let us be too late.

It felt like I was waiting in the car for hours before the state trooper came back.

"Did you find Todd?" I asked.

"No. Stay down." He started the car's engine. "I'm going to take you home. We'll get your story one more time, and then we're going to do everything we can to find your friend, I promise."

When we drove around the corner, he told me it was okay to sit up.

"Was the man home?"

The state trooper nodded.

"Are you going to make him tell you where Todd is?"

"Not quite that simple."

What happened, as I found out later, is that the man was home. I had the right guy—they showed me pictures of several men close to his description, and I picked the correct one. Gerald Martin. Fifty-three years old. Single. Never married. Construction worker.

He was cooperative. Allowed them to search his home without a warrant, as long as they promised not to make too big of a mess. He was, I'm told, more concerned about the missing boy than maintaining his own innocence. He did not own a silver car.

Mr. Martin did not have an alibi beyond, "I was sleeping." It was one in the morning. That was perfectly reasonable.

None of the neighbors had heard anything. Again, it was one in the morning. How often are people awoken from a sound sleep by their neighbor leaving the house or coming home? Especially if he was being discreet about it?

About half an hour had passed between the car driving off with Todd and us arriving at Mr. Martin's house. Thirty minutes for him to get rid of the silver car and get back home. In that thirty minutes he'd also have to subdue—or kill—my best friend.

The math didn't seem that far-fetched to me, but even as a not-quite-fourteen year-old I understood that it would be a hard sell to a jury unless they found evidence directly linking him to the abduction. I was one hundred percent positive that he'd been the one to drive off with Todd. I'd seen him. It was not a trick of my imagination or simply me not seeing him clearly through the car window. Gerald Martin was the one who did it.

Unfortunately, I was a thirteen-year-old kid with a below

average behavior record at school. A solid B-student. Me *swearing* that it was him wasn't enough to overcome the fact that he did not own a silver car, that he'd graciously allowed his home to be searched that very night, and that my eyewitness testimony was literally the only thing connecting him to Todd's disappearance. Plus, I'd been wearing a mask. I knew that I could see perfectly fine with it on, but it was one more way somebody could tear apart my story.

Oh, they took my accusation seriously, and they kept investigating him. Nobody tried to claim that Todd had run away from home. Mr. Martin had covered his tracks very well, apart from not anticipating that his victim's best friend had been hiding in the woods at the time of the abduction.

He was not arrested.

Residents were asked to call with any information they might have. A couple of people did, but the leads went nowhere.

As a minor, I was not part of any of the publicity for the case. I was "an anonymous eyewitness," with no hint given about my age.

Mr. Martin hadn't seen my face. In theory, he had no idea who I was.

Unless he'd forced Todd to tell him.

My parents forbade me to leave the yard by myself, but I wouldn't have gone out even with their permission. I barely went outside at all. It seemed unlikely that he'd drive up to me in broad daylight, drag me into his car, and stab me to death, but I couldn't rule that out.

A month passed. The search continued, though everybody pretty much knew that it was a lost cause by now. I turned fourteen but didn't feel like having a birthday party. My mom still made me a chocolate cake, and I ate a couple of bites and blew out the candles so she wouldn't feel that her efforts to make me feel better were a waste. But it seemed truly horrible to be celebrating getting one year older when I didn't know what kind of nightmarish end Todd might have met. If he was dead, and he almost certainly was, I hoped it had at least been quick. If Mr. Martin was in a hurry to get back to his house, he might have killed him in a fast, painless way rather than taking his sadistic time.

So what I'm saying is that it was a truly miserable summer.

And then, in the middle of August, another boy went missing. A fifth grader this time. He disappeared in North Pole, by which I do not mean the earth's actual north pole, but rather North Pole, Alaska, a very small town less than a twenty-minute drive from Fairbanks. It's where you'll find the Santa Claus House, which has been sending out letters from Santa with a North Pole postmark since 1952. If a child sends a letter to Santa Claus addressed only to the North Pole, that's where they go.

I did not have a speck of evidence that Mr. Martin was responsible. The circumstances weren't the same; right after lunch, the boy had walked to a nearby park to meet some friends and never arrived there. The friends had assumed that he got grounded or something and didn't think much of it, and in the age before cell phones, his parents had no idea that anything was wrong until he didn't come home for dinner. Nobody saw a man with his description in the area. Nobody reported a silver car driving slowly alongside young children. None of Mr. Martin's neighbors had noticed any unusual behavior.

But I knew for a goddamn fact that Mr. Martin had taken Todd. And it was really weird to have three boys go missing like that in a single summer. I assure you, I didn't *want* to confront him. Yet I also didn't want a fourth kid to go missing. Or a fifth. Or a sixth.

I needed to get him to confess. And if that didn't work, or I felt like I was in danger, I'd shoot him. A scenario where I killed Mr. Martin would be better than one where I did nothing and he continued to abduct kids. Perhaps he was innocent in the two other disappearances, but unless he had a twin brother that he hadn't bothered to tell anybody about, he was *not* innocent in Todd's. I had the right guy.

And so I bought the untraceable gun.

When I got home, I took it out of my backpack and hid it under my bed. It probably won't surprise you to discover that my bedroom was not an antiseptic environment in which every object was in its proper place. After many years of going to war over this issue, my parents finally said that they didn't care what my room looked like as long as I didn't leave food in there to rot. I had no reason to believe that anybody searched my room on a regular basis, so I was comfortable with the idea of just keeping the gun under my bed for one night.

I slept horribly. I never remember my dreams, but I kept waking up thinking that the gun was going to go off, shooting right through my mattress into the back of my head. Or into my spine, paralyzing me, so I'd have to lie there helplessly until my mom or dad came in to check on me.

I got up when I heard my parents moving around downstairs. They seemed surprised to see me, since I was normally a lazy piece of crap who didn't get up until after they'd gone to work. For the past couple of summers I'd demonstrated my responsibility by mowing lawns, but I hadn't been doing much of that since Todd went missing.

My mom worked as a bank teller. And if you're thinking, "Wait, didn't he say earlier that his dad was distrustful of banks?" yes, I sure did. Very awkward. My dad was the manager at a furniture store, so we got great deals on furniture, which obviously should have made me the most popular kid at school, yet somehow didn't.

We ate oatmeal together, then they left for work. As soon as the door closed, my stomach began to hurt from the task that awaited me.

I didn't actually know that Mr. Martin was home. I hadn't spent weeks stalking him, learning his schedule and habits like a professional assassin. I just figured that as a construction worker, he might not stick to a standard nine-to-five Monday-through-Friday workweek. If he wasn't home, I'd come back another time.

I wrote a note to my parents, explaining where I'd gone, and left it on the dining room table. I had no intention of them ever seeing this note. When I got home, I'd throw it away. The note was only there in case I didn't come home.

Then I tried to figure out where to put the gun. I hadn't anticipated that this would be a difficult task—I'd just stick the gun in the waistband of my pants, right? The problem was that I wasn't acquiring new clothes at the same rate that I was putting on weight, and even with a sweater (and why would I be wearing a sweater in August?) you could see the bulge. I could've worn a jacket, which would pose the same "Why is he wearing that?" question as a sweater, and if Mr. Martin offered to take my jacket and I refused, he'd know I was hiding something.

Not to mention that a few tests made it clear that I couldn't yank it out of my tight pants at lightning speed. If I actually needed to use it, he would not stand there politely waiting for me to fumble with my firearm. And having the gun wedged in there filled me with the intense fear that it would go off, even though I quadruple checked that the safety was on.

So I'd have to keep the gun in my backpack. This wasn't ideal, but I'd keep my backpack with me the entire time, mostly unzipped, and I'd make sure I knew exactly where the gun was.

I tested it a few times. Reached in and grabbed the gun as quickly as I could. Nobody would ever come up with a catchy nickname honoring my fast-draw abilities, but I was confident that, if necessary, I could pull the gun on him in time.

The confession presented another problem.

Microcassette recorders *might* have been around in 1979, but I sure didn't have one, nor did anybody I knew. We had big, clunky tape recorders. Though technically it would fit in my backpack, I couldn't shove it under some other stuff like I did the gun or it would be too muffled to record anything. And if I was there longer than half an hour, it would shut off with a loud snap, which would be extremely inconvenient.

Thus, I couldn't present a recorded confession to the authorities. I just had to get something I could use against him. A confession obtained at gunpoint wouldn't be admissible in court, but my goal was to force him to give me proof about what he'd done.

And if I couldn't make that happen, I'd kill him.

I rode my bicycle over to his house, hoping he wouldn't be home.

A car was in the driveway. The same car that had been there when I brought the state trooper over.

I stared at the house for a long time, trying to work up my courage.

I finally accepted that there was not going to be a moment where I *wanted* to do this. I just had to walk up there and knock on the door.

Feeling like I was going to throw up, pass out, and wet my pants, I went up to his front door. I stood there for a moment, sweating. Then I knocked.

Gerald Martin answered the door.

4

He frowned when he saw me.

He hadn't seen my face on the night of the abduction, but he might know who I was. Todd and I weren't very popular. It wouldn't take a whole lot of sleuthing to discover that we were best friends. Seeing Mr. Martin behind the wheel of that car was permanently seared into my memory, and if he had a clear memory of looking at me, he'd know my hair color and body type. I'd knocked on his door knowing perfectly well that he might immediately realize who was standing there.

"Yes?" he asked. His tone was annoyed. More "Why are you bothering me, kid?" than "It's *you!*"

"Hello," I said. "I'm Curtis Black."

"Okay."

"I wanted to call, but you're not in the phone book."

"That's right. There's a reason for that." Mr. Martin scratched his chin. He was fully dressed in jeans and a plain white T-shirt, but he hadn't shaved and, from the smell of him, hadn't bathed. I could see a tan line around his neck. He had the lean but muscular build of somebody who spent his days working outside.

"I apologize for that," I told him. "I was wondering if I could interview you."

"About what?"

"About you. I have a school assignment where I'm supposed to interview somebody and write an essay about them."

"School's out."

"They give us work to do over the summer." This wasn't true, but would a childless construction worker know that? My cousins in Ohio said they got a summer reading list, so this didn't seem completely out of the realm of possibility.

"Then interview your mom."

"We're not allowed to interview relatives. That would be too easy. It's supposed to be somebody we don't know."

"Why me?"

I had toyed with the idea of making up something, like wanting to interview him about what steps were involved in paving a road. But when I made the final decision that I was really going to do this, I decided to stick to the truth as much as possible, to decrease the chances that he'd figure out that I was a lying little weasel trying to get him to confess to a trio of murders. "You were falsely accused of kidnapping Todd Lester. I thought that would be an interesting interview. Most of my friends are picking really lame subjects."

"Such as?"

"Excuse me?"

"What really lame subjects are your friends picking?"

I honestly hadn't expected him to question me on something like this, and my mind suddenly went blank. I hoped my eyes didn't go wide. "Y'know," I said, "teachers and stuff."

"Your friends are interviewing teachers?"

"Yes."

"You're right. That sounds boring." This *seemed* like a comment that would be accompanied by a smile, but it wasn't.

"And one of my friends is interviewing a barber. Another one is interviewing the guy who owns the bowling alley." Was I giving too much information? I was definitely giving too much information. I needed to shut up now.

"Which bowling alley?"

"Arctic Bowl."

"Okay."

"I didn't know there was another one."

"I don't know if there is or not. I don't bowl."

"I do sometimes," I said.

Mr. Martin said nothing.

"Anyway, would it be all right if I interviewed you?" I asked.

"It sounds like your friends are interviewing people about their jobs."

"They are. Most of them are. But the assignment doesn't say we have to do that. We can interview them about anything."

Mr. Martin stared at me for too long of a moment. "Do I get to read your essay before you turn it in?"

"Yeah, sure, of course."

"All right."

Though he'd said "All right," he just continued to stand in his doorway and stare at me, as if waiting for me to make the first move.

"I was hoping to do it now, but I can come back later," I said.

"When's it due?"

"Next week."

"Procrastinator, huh?"

"Yeah."

"Come on in," he said. "Place is a mess."

"That's okay."

I switched my backpack, which felt extremely heavy, from my left shoulder to my right as I followed him through the doorway into his living room. Gerald Martin had a *very* different definition of "Place is a mess" than I did. As far as I could tell, he meant that he hadn't vacuumed in the past half hour. I'm not suggesting that he'd wiped everything down with bleach while ranting about being able to see the germs slithering over his skin, but Mr. Martin was a very tidy housekeeper.

The place was way less creepy that I'd expected. Obviously, I'd known that there wouldn't be severed human heads mounted upon the wall, but I'd expected maybe a caribou head, its face frozen in terror. Or disturbing artwork that he'd painted himself. *Something* that was "off," something to make me say, "Yes, the man who lives here is definitely the kind of person who abducts teenaged boys."

But it was a normal house. Sparsely furnished, yet not sparsely enough to feel weird. Though I wouldn't go so far as to say that it had a welcoming feel, I didn't feel like I was walking into the lair of a predator.

"Sit down," he told me. It wasn't quite a command, but also not quite a friendly offer for me to make myself at home.

I was extremely self-conscious about my backpack as I sat down on the couch—I had this vision of a prominent gun-shaped bulge on the side. I unzipped the backpack, took out a notebook, then set the backpack on the carpet next to my feet without zipping it up again.

"Want a glass of water?" he asked.

"Oh, no, thank you," I said. My throat went dry as I said it, and I barely got the last word out. I coughed.

"I'll get you a glass of water," he said.

He walked out of the living room. He was probably going to be gone long enough for me to take the gun out of my backpack and shove it between the couch cushions for easier access, but if he heard the rustling and poked his head back into the room, that would be outrageously bad. Instead, I just sat there, hoping I wasn't sweating too much.

Maybe I should abandon this insane plan. Apologize for bothering him and get the hell out of here.

Then how would I feel when the next kid disappeared?

How *should* I feel? Why was this my responsibility? Why was I, a fourteen-year-old, sitting in the living room of a serial kidnapper? Getting into a fight with Todd and causing him to walk home by himself didn't mean that I was obligated to put myself at risk for being murdered—or worse—did it?

I would be well within my moral rights to say, "Hey, I'm just a kid!" and not get involved.

But I was here, on his couch, with a gun in my backpack, and I was going to see this through…while making every possible effort to ensure that I did not become his next victim.

I sat there as I heard the faucet turn on in the kitchen.

It turned off.

Mr. Martin walked back into the living room. Without a word, he set a glass of water, only half full, on the coffee table in front of me.

"Thank you," I said, even though there wasn't a chance in hell that I'd drink anything he offered to me.

"Are you hot?" he asked.

"No, why?"

"You're sweating."

"Oh. Yeah, I got hot when I walked here."

"Don't you own a bicycle?"

He asked it like an innocent question, no trace of menace that I could detect. But I'd walked here because he might recognize my bicycle from that night.

"Yeah," I said. "I'm trying to get in shape."

"You can get in shape with a bicycle."

"I know. I heard walking's better."

Mr. Martin nodded. He sat down on a wooden rocking chair that faced the couch, though he did not rock. "How's this going to work?"

I slid the pencil out of the metal spiral on my notebook. "I'm just going to ask you a few questions. It shouldn't take very long." My mouth went dry again, but I tried to hide it. I didn't want him to urge me to take a drink of water.

"All right."

"Your name is Gerald Martin, right?"

"Yes."

I wrote it down. "Spelled just like it sounds?"

"Yes."

"Where and when were you born?"

"Los Angeles, California, in 1926."

"Why did you move to Fairbanks?"

"I like the cold. And I like that it's far away from everything."

I wrote that down as well. If he asked to look at my notebook, he'd see legitimate notes taken about our interview.

"What happened on the night that Todd Lester disappeared?"

"I don't know," said Mr. Martin. "I've never even met him."

"I mean, what happened to you?"

"I got woken up around one-thirty by a knock at the door. A state trooper. A nice enough guy, considering that he was waking me up to accuse me of kidnapping a kid I'd never even met. It wasn't like I had to get up at six to go to work or anything, right? I told him that I didn't know anything about it, and that he was welcome to look around my house even though he didn't have a search warrant. Are you getting this? Should I slow down?"

"I'm getting it," I said, frantically scribbling.

"Are you sure? I don't want to read this paper and find out that I've been misquoted."

"You won't be."

"I'm trusting you."

"Like I said, you'll get to read it before I turn it in."

"You live over in Gulfstream Acres, don't you?"

"Yeah."

"I'm not sure you ever told me your name."

"I did. Curtis Black."

"Oh, that's right. Go on."

"Did anything else happen that night?" I asked.

"Some more state troopers showed up. Searched my place. Left it a mess even though I specifically asked them to be respectful, since I was letting them do it without a warrant. They didn't find anything, of course. Every once in a while they come back to ask me more questions and harass me some more. All my neighbors think I did it. And now I've got kids coming to interview me about it. I should've stayed in L.A."

"How long have you been here?"

"Three years."

"I'm not here to interview you because I think you did it," I assured him. "My interview is about what it's like to be falsely accused."

"You didn't write down the three years," Mr. Martin told me.

I wrote it down. "Why do they think it was you?"

"My neighbors? Because the cops keep showing up at my door to chat."

"I meant the cops."

"They don't *think* it's me. I'm just on their list of suspects. A very short list. Personally, I think it was his parents, but that's off the record. You know what 'off the record' means, right?"

"Yes," I said.

"It means don't put it in your paper."

"I know. I won't."

"I try to keep to myself and make an honest living. I don't bother anybody. The assholes at the end of the block have loud parties every Friday night, blasting the shittiest music you can imagine, crap that I wouldn't force a dog to listen to, but I'm the creepy villain around here."

"Do people say anything to you?"

"Would you come up and talk to me if you believed that I murdered some kids?"

"I guess not."

Mr. Martin shook his head. "They don't say anything. Yeah, a couple of guys at work tried to start some shit, but I shut that down real quick. Still, everybody looks at me. I know what they're thinking. You know that I didn't actually get arrested, right?"

"Yeah."

"They didn't even take me into the station. They've got nothing. Either somebody else took Todd Lester, or he ran away. He's either dead or in Anchorage."

"Okay."

"You stopped writing again."

"I thought we were still off the record."

"Were you friends with Todd?"

"Yeah."

"Close friends?"

"Yeah."

"Best friends?"

I shrugged.

"We can go back on the record again," he said.

"I think I've got what I need," I told him. This had been a spectacularly bad idea. I honestly couldn't even remember the many clever ways I'd planned to trap him in a lie. All I could think of now was that it would be in my best interest to get the hell out of his house as soon as possible.

"Excuse me?"

"This should do it."

"That's it?"

"Yes," I said, standing up. "I've got enough."

"No, no, no," said Mr. Martin. "You didn't interrupt me on my day off for a half-assed interview. You're going to turn in an A-paper that we both can be proud of. Ask me another question."

"It doesn't have to be a very long paper."

"Sit down and ask me another question." He was able to convey the tone of shouting without actually raising his voice.

I sat back down on the couch. The moment my butt hit the cushion, I decided that I should've just fled for the door. Taken my chances that I could get out of the house before he grabbed me by the shirt collar and threw me to the floor.

I struggled to come up with something to ask. "Do you, uh, do you think you'll stay around here?"

"Ask me a better question."

My mind was completely blank. Was I in danger? Should I go for the gun?

"Why were you a suspect?" I asked, and then immediately regretted it.

"That's a very good, interesting question." Mr. Martin leaned forward in the rocking chair. "Somebody told the police that I was the one who did it. That's all they have. An unreliable eyewitness."

"Okay."

"Are you planning to become a journalist, Curtis?"

"I don't know. No. Not really."

"I can tell. Because this is when you ask what they call 'a follow-up' question. Do you know what that means?"

"Yeah, of course."

"Then ask a follow-up question."

I couldn't think of one. And when I tried to admit that I couldn't think of one, I couldn't speak, either.

"It's not that hard," said Mr. Martin. "If you're trying to get the full story for your paper, ask me if I know who told the police that I kidnapped Todd Lester."

"Do you know?"

Mr. Martin shook his head. "No. I don't. They wouldn't tell me."

"Oh."

"Since you're not doing a very good job with the questions, do you mind if I ask you one?"

"Sure," I said.

"What's your favorite Halloween costume?"

"I don't know."

"Of course you do. You're not too old to trick or treat, are you? Maybe you are. I don't know when kids stop. But you had a favorite Halloween costume in the past, right? Spider-Man, maybe? That gold robot from *Star Wars*? Something scary? A skeleton? A vampire? What was it?"

I should go for the gun. But I couldn't make my arm move.

"I asked you a question," said Mr. Martin. "If you're not going to ask me questions, you can at least answer the ones I ask you."

"I guess Spider-Man," I told him.

"Good guess on my part, then. When did you dress as Spider-Man for Halloween? Last year? The year before? When you were six?"

"I don't remember."

"Try to remember."

"When I was eight, maybe."

"You dressed as Spider-Man for Halloween when you were eight years old. I bet you were adorable. I'd like to see the Polaroids. Now I'm going to be a good journalist and ask you a follow-up question. Are you ready?"

"Yeah."

"How old were you when you went as a mouse?"

5

I did everything I possibly could to keep my expression neutral. I'd gone through countless scenarios in my mind before I showed up here, and most of them included a moment where Mr. Martin figured out that I was the little bastard who'd ratted him out.

In those scenarios, I thrust my hand into my backpack, grabbed the gun, and pointed it at him before he knew what was happening.

Now, in the actual moment, I doubted my ability to whip out the gun in time. I'd be fumbling around in there while he casually walked over and slashed my throat with the knife he'd probably stashed in his pocket while he was getting my glass of water. I also doubted my ability to actually shoot another human being, even an evil one. In my imagination, I'd opened fire with deadly accuracy, hitting him a few times in the chest and sending him flying across the room, with about as much blood as you'd see in a PG-rated movie. In real life, I suddenly knew that it would be ugly. Awful. I'd never recover.

Mr. Martin had not stood up from the rocking chair.

Even if he rushed at me, I could probably get the gun. I was quick. I'd practiced.

This was why I was here. Not to run off like a coward, with absolutely nothing to show for this botched plan except the certainty that a psychopath now knew who I was.

I couldn't make myself reach for the backpack. Maybe that was for the best. Maybe my uncooperative muscles were being controlled by the part of my brain that didn't want me to make a fatal mistake.

I just had to pray that my face hadn't given anything away.

I'd play dumb.

"Mighty Mouse?" I asked.

"Maybe," said Mr. Martin. "Some cartoon mouse."

"I've never been a mouse for Halloween."

"Never?"

"Never."

"You sure?"

"Of course I'm sure. I'd remember."

"You don't own a mouse mask?"

"No."

Mr. Martin nodded. He didn't look like he believed me.

Had he somehow walked into a trap that I'd failed to set? I'd blundered my way through this conversation without cleverly catching him in an inconsistency in his story, but had he been told about my mask? None of the news articles, and I'd read all of them, identified the witness as "a chubby kid in a mouse mask." Would anybody have shared that detail with him? Had he just admitted to having information he shouldn't have known?

And would that be sufficient? If I went back and said, "Hey, he knew what kind of mask I was wearing!" would that be enough to get him arrested?

What if they *had* told him? I wasn't privy to any of the

conversations he'd had with the authorities. Maybe they'd shared that with him. I couldn't think of any possible reason that they would, especially since they were trying to protect my identity, but I wasn't an expert on those kinds of things.

Should I confront him with this?

Did I want to be sitting a few feet away from a serial killer when he realized that he fucked up?

After a split second of indecision, I decided to compromise. I would not point out that Mr. Martin shouldn't know about the mask—which might be a suicidal move—but I wouldn't try to leave. I'd get more information to use against him. He'd proven that he could make a mistake.

"How many times have you been questioned?" I asked.

"I thought you said you had enough information for your paper."

"I thought you said I didn't."

Mr. Martin shrugged. "That's a boring question. The answer is just a number. If you want to impress your teacher, find out how I *feel* about being unfairly targeted. Capture the emotional impact of the story."

I tried to speak but once again my voice failed me. Ironic, considering how often I got in trouble for speaking when I wasn't supposed to. I coughed.

He stood up.

Walked over to me.

Picked up the glass of water, took a drink, and set it back down.

"See?" he said. "It's fine. No poison. No drugs." He walked back to his rocking chair and sat down.

"I didn't think there was," I managed to say. I still didn't want to drink the water. He might not have put anything in it, but I didn't want to drink from the same glass as the man who'd killed my best friend.

"Well, I can't force you to drink. I'd offer you something else, but all I've got is beer in the fridge. Pretty sure your mommy and daddy wouldn't appreciate that."

"At least not this early in the morning," I said.

Mr. Martin stared at me for a moment.

"Was that a joke?" he asked.

"Yeah."

"Not bad."

"Thanks."

"Is humor your defense mechanism?"

"Sometimes, yeah."

"I figured. You're all sweaty and inarticulate, but you can make a joke. Feeling like you need a defense mechanism now, huh? Why are you so scared?"

"I'm not scared," I insisted.

"Oh, come on, Curtis. I know what fear looks like."

I wiped some sweat from my forehead. "I'm just hot."

"It's not hot in here. And I get it, fat kids sweat a lot, but you've just been sitting there. I'm sure you've recuperated from your vigorous walk by now. You seem flustered. Why? You're the one who knocked on my door. Do you think I kidnapped your buddy? Is that what this is all about?"

"No."

"If I called your school, would somebody be able to confirm your homework assignment?"

I made a point of looking him directly in the eye. "Yes." He was bluffing. He wouldn't actually call the school. And if he did, I'd get the hell out of here while he was flipping through the phone book.

"All right," he said. He rocked the chair back and forth, just once. "I told you to find the emotional impact of the story, but maybe when you write it up you should focus on your own emotions. Make the story about you. How scared you were, sitting in my living room, talking to the man that you thought took your friend away from you."

"I don't think it's you."

"You absolutely think it's me."

"I wouldn't be here if I did."

Mr. Martin smiled. "I'm not as smart as your teachers, but I'm smarter than a teenager. I'm a suspect in three different disappearances. That's got to be scary for somebody like you, who fits the profile of the missing kids. So if I thought you were really here to do an interview for a summer assignment, I'd say, well, sure, of course he's nervous, that makes total sense. But I don't believe that's why you're here. You're trying to play amateur detective. You think you're Encyclopedia Brown or the Hardy Boys. You think you're going to solve The Mystery of the Disappearing Kids. Be a great big hero all around Fairbanks."

"That's not it at all," I said.

"No? Then is it revenge?"

"It's a school paper."

"You keep saying that, and you keep sweating like a goddamn pig. Look at yourself. It's disgusting. Just being across the room from you makes me want to take a shower. No girl will ever want some overweight boyfriend that she has to towel off before she gets near him. Stop eating so much junk food. Play a sport or something. What did you think you were going to do, get a confession out of me? You've got the wrong guy. Now why don't you just run along home before you waste even more of my time?"

This is where I could have simply stood up and walked out of his house.

That would have been the safe way to play this.

But just as Mr. Martin was convinced—correctly—that I was lying about the assignment, I was more certain than ever that he was the driver of the car. His knowledge about the mask was *something*, but possibly not enough to prove his guilt. I had to get more out of him.

"How'd you know about the mouse mask?" I asked.

I hoped for a flicker of doubt. Just a flicker.

Instead, I got another smile. "One of the state troopers told me. I'm sure he wasn't supposed to. It turns out they can be kind of sloppy. You thought you caught me in a mistake, didn't you?"

"I was just wondering."

"You're a surprisingly bad liar. When I was your age, I lied all the damn time. Why are you so terrible at it? Don't you ever lie to your parents about where you've been?"

I'm not sure what he intended to accomplish with his attitude, but I was becoming less anxious and more pissed off. Not that I was going to rush at him and try to claw his eyes out, but the idea of politely excusing myself and going home was losing its appeal. He abducted Todd. Probably killed him. And I'd make sure he didn't get away with it.

"Fine," I said. "I think you did it."

"Now we're getting somewhere. What makes you say that?"

"I saw you."

"And you don't think it's possible that you were mistaken?"

"Do you have a twin brother?" I asked.

"No."

"Then it was you."

"You sound pretty certain of this."

"I am."

"I wasn't there, so I don't know the whole story," said Mr. Martin. "The way I understand it, the witness didn't get close enough to press his face against the windows and peer inside. He saw the events from a distance. While he was wearing a mask, for some unknown reason. When you go trick-or-treating with your little friends, how well do you see through those narrow eyeholes?"

"I see fine. It's not a blindfold."

"What are you hoping for here, Curtis? Think I'll just spill my guts?"

"Maybe. If you know you're caught."

"You're wasting your time. I was fast asleep that night—at least until the state trooper woke me up. I'm heartsick over your friend's disappearance, what his parents must be going through, what *you* must be going through, and I pray that he'll find his way home. All you're doing is harassing a hard-working, honest citizen."

"I thought of a follow-up question," I said.

"Let's hear it."

"You were going to call my school to see if the assignment was real. If I call the cops who talked to you, will they verify that they told you about the mask?"

"Yep."

"Should we do it?"

"No," said Mr. Martin.

"Why not? Because you know they'll say you're lying?"

"Because you haven't earned my trust. What's to stop you from telling them that I'm holding you here against your will? I shouldn't have let you in my home in the first place. In fact, I'd like you to leave now."

"May I ask one more follow-up question?"

"Go ahead."

"What the fuck did you do to my friend?"

"Oooh, the tone has changed," said Mr. Martin. "I'm not sure if I like it or not. Let me be perfectly clear, Curtis. If I *was* the person you're looking for, if I'd lured poor Todd into my car, sawed off his arms and legs, and thrown his body into the Chena River, I can *assure* you that you wouldn't get that information out of me by faking a school assignment. If I was the guilty party, which I'm not, do you think I could fool the authorities, the people who devote their entire lives to catching criminals…and yet you're going to stumble on in here and catch me red-handed? Is that seriously what you thought? Do you think you're some kind of genius, Curtis? That wasn't a rhetorical question. I'd like to know. Do you think you're some kind of genius?"

"No."

"Good. Because from where I sit, you're rock-stupid. Which is a real problem for you, because you're clearly not athletic, so you need brains to balance out your weak blob of a body. I know the assignment doesn't exist, but you should write it up anyway. Write up an entire paper about what an idiot you were for doing this. I figure you'll get a C, maybe a C-minus. Not too bad for somebody as dumb as you."

I wondered if Mr. Martin would talk to me like this if he knew I had a handgun in my backpack.

"And I'll be perfectly happy if you call the state troopers. Go ahead and tell them I was rude to you. Send them back over here. See how harassing a private citizen, one who hasn't been charged with any crime, works out for you."

"Why are you so nervous?" I asked.

"What the fuck makes you think I'm nervous?"

"You're talking a lot. I'm just a fat little kid. Why are you wasting your time having this discussion with me? If you think I'm making up the assignment, why are we still sitting here? Why haven't you kicked me out of your house?"

"I asked you to leave."

"And then you started ranting."

"*Now* it's time for you to go."

"And if I don't?" I knew that this was getting out of hand. Hell, Mr. Martin might have a hidden gun of his own within easy reach. But he'd flipped a switch inside of me, and I wanted him to be exposed for the monster he was. If I could keep him angry—but hopefully not *homicidally* angry—I might get the information I needed out of him.

Mr. Martin stood up. "Then I'll remove you."

It might have been possible for me to simply get up and head for the door. He might not have tried to stop me. Or, he might have forcibly shoved me out the door, not bothering with the throat-slitting. Reviewing my decision with a few decades of hindsight, I'm still not certain what advice I would give to my fourteen-year-old self in this moment. If I could have paused time, sat there on the couch with an unlimited opportunity to really consider my next move, I don't know what course of action I'd have arrived upon, but I kind of think I would have decided: *go for the gun.*

Which is what I did.

I thrust my hand into my backpack.

Mr. Martin raised his eyebrows, looking confused. Had it never occurred to him to wonder what was in there? Had he assumed that he was in complete control of the situation?

I'd practiced. I should, in theory, have been able to pull out the gun before he closed the distance between us. Shoved it in his face just as he reached me.

My hand went straight to the handle of the weapon.

Mr. Martin moved forward.

I pulled out the gun. All of that practice had paid off. That part of the plan was flawless.

Mr. Martin hadn't even made it halfway across the living room before I pointed the gun at him. The next move, which I'd also practiced, was to flick off the safety with my thumb.

He just stood there, staring at me.

"Well, shit," he finally said.

6

I kept the gun pointed at him as I got up off the couch. "Sit back down," I told him.

"Where?" Mr. Martin asked.

"Where do you think? Back in your chair. Don't play stupid with me."

Mr. Martin sat back down in the rocking chair. He didn't look frightened or angry—he looked more *bewildered* that this had happened to him. "Planning to kill me?"

"I hope not." My hands were trembling a bit, but not so badly that I was in danger of dropping the gun. I didn't care if he noticed.

"Then what do you want?"

This was the part of the conversation I'd actually rehearsed out loud, fine-tuning it to make sure I sounded as cold-blooded as possible. I wanted him to know that he could not reason with me. I was in control. "I want information," I told him. "I want you to tell me exactly what happened that night, and what you did with Todd after you drove away. I'll know if you're lying. The first lie, I'll shoot you in the leg. The second lie, I'll shoot you in the face. Have I made myself completely clear?"

Mr. Martin gave just the hint of a smile. "Goddamn, kid. You sound like a complete sociopath."

"Have I made myself completely clear?" I repeated. I was speaking perfectly now—no need for a drink of water.

"Yeah, we're clear. But have you thought this through? We're not out in the middle of the forest. Neighbors will hear the gunshot. They'll hear me screaming in pain. You're only fourteen, but since you showed up here with a gun they'll know this was completely premeditated. You'll be tried as an adult. You could get the electric chair."

"If that happens, it won't be your problem. You'll be dead." I had indeed thought about that, which is why I'd lied to him: the first shot would not be in his leg. There would be no screaming. Maybe somebody would hear the gun go off, or maybe the neighbors were all at work. Either way, the occasional sound of a gunshot was not unusual around here, and my family, at least, had never dialed 911 when we heard one.

"Do you know what the electric chair is like?" he asked. "It's not just a quick zap and you're dead. It's the most unbelievable pain you can imagine shooting through your body. It doesn't always finish you off the first time. Sometimes they have to pull the lever a few times. You'll shit your pants. Right there in front of all the witnesses. That'll be how they remember you—face covered with drool, sitting in a pile of your own baked shit."

I fully extended the arm with the gun toward him. "From now on, you only talk when I tell you to. You're not going to get out of this by making up some ridiculous story about how they'll send a kid to the chair."

"It's not—"

"Did you really just talk already?"

Mr. Martin closed his mouth.

"The first question is going to be yes or no. I'm going to be watching you very closely. I've spent the whole summer researching the signs that somebody isn't telling the truth. If you lie to me, I will pull this trigger. Are you completely clear on how this is going to work?"

"Was that the first question?"

I lunged forward with the gun, just a bit. Mr. Martin flinched.

He was scared. Good.

"Again, are you completely clear on how this is going to work? Yes or no?"

"Yes."

"Did you abduct Todd Lester?"

He was silent for a moment. "Yes."

I suddenly wanted to burst into tears, but I kept myself under control. Now I needed to get enough details out of him that the authorities could prove his guilt. "How did you get him in your car?"

"I told him that his dad fell and cracked open his skull, and that his mom was in the emergency room, and that she was so frantic and scared that I'd offered to pick him up and take him there."

"What was his reaction?"

"He started crying and got in."

I didn't want to ask this next question. I was sure I already knew the answer. "Is he dead?"

Mr. Martin sighed.

"I asked you if he's dead. Yes or no?"

"What do you want me to tell you? That he's happy and healthy?"

"I want the truth."

"Yes, he's dead."

Once again I resisted the urge to burst into tears. "Did he suffer?"

Mr. Martin sighed again. He looked at the floor. "Depends on what you mean by suffer."

"You know what the word suffer means."

"Are you asking if it hurt? Yeah, it fuckin' hurt. Did it go on and on and on? No. Five minutes at the most."

"How did you do it?"

"A knife. You want the brand? You want me to see if we can find it in the Sears catalog? You want me to describe every detail of his final moments? I can probably do a pretty good impression of how his voice sounded, the things he said to me, but you don't want that in your head. I don't like having it in mine, and I'm the one who did it."

"Was he already dead when the state trooper got there?"

"No."

"When did you kill him?"

"A couple days later."

"Why did you wait so long?"

"It wasn't safe."

"What kind of car were you driving?"

"A 1974 Datsun 260Z."

"What color?"

"Silver."

"Where is it now?" I asked.

"Dismantled."

"Where was it that night?"

"A garage. Why are we doing this? Why don't you just call the police?" He gestured toward the kitchen. "The phone's in there. On the wall next to the refrigerator."

"Do you think I'm stupid?"

"What, you think I'm lying about the phone? You think it's out of the realm of possibility that I've got a phone mounted on the wall in there?"

"I think it's out of the realm of possibility that you'll still be here when I get back."

"Well, shit, then march me on in there with you. Whack me in the back of the head with the gun if you think it'll keep me in line. You won, okay? Game, set, match. You're the victor. I accept that. So all I care about right now is making sure you don't shoot me, either accidentally or on purpose."

"I'll decide when it's time to call the police," I told him.

"Fine."

"Why were you driving around that night?"

"I have trouble sleeping. I'm exhausted when I fall into bed but I just can't shut off my brain. Driving around sometimes relaxes me." Mr. Martin's voice had changed a bit, as if it was a relief to be able to speak freely about this stuff. "On that particular night, all I wanted to do was drive around for half an hour or so and then go back home, but I saw an opportunity and took it. I didn't sleep well that night, in case you were wondering."

"Did you kill the other two?"

"Which two?"

"You know who I'm talking about."

Mr. Martin nodded.

"Were there others?"

"You mean in Alaska?"

"Anywhere."

"A couple."

"Do you specifically mean that there were two more?"

"Yes," said Mr. Martin. "A couple means two. Otherwise I

would have said 'a few.' They weren't from around here, if that was your next question."

"Do you have any remorse?" I asked. Damn. I was getting off track. This question was irrelevant—I wanted details that could prove his guilt, not the story of how his father locked him in the basement with rats every time he misbehaved. I needed to focus.

"Do I have any remorse?" Mr. Martin sounded legitimately shocked that I'd asked him this question. "I have nothing *but* remorse. You think I like being this way? Every single minute of every single day is hell on earth. I haven't had a genuine moment of happiness in…I don't even know how long. If we could trade places —if you could be inside my head for just three seconds—you couldn't be able to cope with it. You'd go straight to the goddamn fetal position and you might never get up. Trust me, I hate myself far worse than you hate me."

I wasn't convinced of that, but it didn't seem like something I should bother to debate.

Was I done? Did I have enough? I wasn't sure if I should keep throwing questions at him, or if I should quit while I was ahead.

"Will it make you feel good to shoot me in the head?" he asked.

"I don't know. Maybe."

"Why draw attention with a gunshot? If you want revenge, why not do it in a way that's safer and more satisfying? Go to the kitchen. Open the drawer next to the sink. You'll find a few knives. Pick the one you like best."

"I'm not here for revenge."

"Bullshit. Of course you are. I totally understand. I'd be here for revenge too, if I were you, and I wish to God that I was. You've got your whole life ahead of you. I've got nothing. Not a damn thing."

"Am I supposed to feel sorry for you?"

"Hell no. You're supposed to feel disgust. You're supposed to want to put me down like a rabid dog. Do you play sports? I can tell that you don't but I thought I'd ask."

"I play sports in gym class."

"Do you play baseball? Softball counts, too."

"Sometimes."

"If you go into my bedroom, and you look in the closet, you'll find a baseball bat. It's a good one. Hard maple—not that aluminum crap they've started using. I will kneel down on the floor, and after you practice your swing a few times, getting it just right, you can crack me on the head as hard as you can. Break my neck. Shatter my skull. That will be so much more satisfying than shooting me, don't you think?"

"I already said that I don't want to kill you."

"Oh, but you do. And the sound of my head splattering won't alert the neighbors. It's so much safer for you. And no matter how mad you get, a gun fails you once it's out of bullets. With a bat, you can keep hitting me and hitting me and hitting me until I'm scattered all over the room and your arms are so sore that they feel like they're going to fall off."

"Time to stop talking now," I said.

"Think how good you'll feel after you do it. Justice served. The good guys won. I'll never hurt another living creature. Now, you can't just leave my corpse here. Even if I'm a bloody gooshy mess, they've got lab people who can do mathematical calculations and shit and trace it back to you. So you'll need to cut up my body. I've got an axe in the shed—the key is hanging on a hook by the back door—and if you put some elbow grease into it, it won't take that long. I've got a chainsaw in there, too, but those are loud and it'll be suspicious to have one running inside my house. Wrap me up—"

"Shut up," I told him.

"I'm not done. This is useful information. Wrap me up in garbage bags. Don't worry about the waste—use more bags than you think you need. One bag for each of my arms and legs, one for my head, and two or three for my chest. Don't put my entire torso in one. It's heavier than you think. Wrap up the axe and the baseball bat, too. Then get some rubber gloves and bleach and scrub, scrub, scrub. Don't just look for the blood. Scrub everything. There'll be tiny particles that you won't see with the naked eye. I live alone, so you don't have to worry about anybody walking in on you. If somebody knocks on the door, just wait until they go away. You don't have a driver's license, so actually getting rid of the body parts will be more challenging. You'll have to make several trips. This is no time to get lazy. Maybe you should get your notebook and write this down."

He rocked the chair forward.

And then he jumped out of it and ran at me.

It's possible that his long speech was entirely intended to get me to lower my defenses. It's also possible that he thought a fourteen-year-old kid who was clearly only *pretending* to be brave might not be able to actually pull the trigger when the moment arrived. Or, hell, maybe he didn't care if I shot him in the head or not. Better than prison. Worth the risk.

The speech did not get me to lower my defenses.

But when he lunged at me, arms outstretched, face full of terrifying rage, my instinct was not to squeeze the trigger. My instinct was to step back away from him. And by the time my brain screamed *Shoot him! Shoot the son of a bitch!* he'd knocked the gun out of my hand.

I'd choked. After all this, I'd fucking choked.

Yes, I was a frightened fourteen-year-old against a serial killer… but I'd had him at gunpoint. I'd *won.* I'd beaten the man who murdered my best friend, and now I was suddenly in danger of sharing Todd's fate.

Mr. Martin punched me in the gut.

I dropped to my knees, gasping for breath.

He picked up the gun.

"Pathetic," he muttered. "You should be more embarrassed than scared. Your friend was counting on you to avenge his death, and you let him down. No soul at rest for him. Absolutely pathetic."

I wanted to say something, yet I couldn't catch my breath and my mind couldn't process exactly *what* I wanted to say.

"Don't piss your pants," he said. "I don't mind cleaning up blood and gore, but piss is just plain gross."

I tried to stand up, but instead tumbled forward, catching my fall with my hands. I continued violently coughing.

"Don't puke either. Can I trust you not to go for the gun if I leave for a second, or do I need to stomp on your hands until every single bone is broken?"

I couldn't answer.

Mr. Martin crouched down next to me. "Nah, I don't think I can trust you. Feeling pretty bad about your recent choices, huh?"

"I—"

"You what?"

"I—"

"Spit it out. These are your last words, so try to make them count. Don't waste them on begging and pleading and degrading yourself. Think of something brave. Something you'd want quoted in the history books. Something that would make President Carter proud. Not that anybody will ever know your last words. Nobody will ever find out what happened to you, not your parents or anybody else, but for your own personal satisfaction, why not try to make your last words count? Make you a deal. If your last words impress me, I'll bury you next to your friend."

"I left a note."

"Okay. Tell me about this note."

"It says where I am."

61

"Oh, yeah?"

I nodded. I stayed on my knees but got back up from a crouched position. "If I'm not home when my parents get there, they'll know exactly what happened to me."

"Well then," said Mr. Martin, "I guess we've got a problem to work out, don't we?"

7

"**M**y parents will be home any minute," I said.

Mr. Martin shook his head. "I believe you when you said you left a note. You seem like a smart enough kid and it makes sense that you'd have a backup plan. I *don't* believe that they'll be home any minute. You wouldn't want them to discover the note while you were still forcing a confession out of me at gunpoint. Honestly, I think that if I killed you right now, I'd have time to find out where you live, break into your house, find the note, and burn it."

"You'll never find it."

"Maybe, maybe not. Lucky for you, I don't feel like going through the trouble. I don't want to kill you when there's already heat on me. That would be fucking stupid. That's what you've got going for you right now—killing you isn't in my best interest."

"I won't say anything to anybody."

"You promise?"

"I swear to God," I said, even though I knew it wouldn't be this simple.

"Uh-huh. Right. You'll be tattling on me the second you feel safe. If this truce is going to work, we need to respect each other's intelligence. Do we agree on that?"

"Yeah." I was perspiring so heavily now that it was dripping into my eyes. The salty liquid burned.

"If we go our separate ways, we both need to keep each other honest. Lucky for you, I've met some pretty damn unsavory people in my life. For example, I have this one close friend who owes me a favor. He does terrible things for money. He's not from around here, but he's happy to travel if you cover his expenses. I'm going to make an arrangement with him that if I get arrested, or if I don't call him at a certain time every day, he is to pay you a little visit."

I vigorously nodded. "Okay, yes." As soon as he'd knocked the gun out of my hand, I'd been one hundred percent convinced that I was going to die. Horribly. So barring a scenario where he gave me my freedom in exchange for luring new victims to his home, I was going to enthusiastically agree to anything he wanted.

"He won't kill you," Mr. Martin explained. "He will *work* on you, with a set of tools that he only takes out for special occasions. You will never wipe your own ass again. You'll only eat through a feeding tube. The only life experiences waiting for you will involve lying in a bed, blinking at people to let them know you understand what they're saying."

My stomach hurt even worse than it did after he punched me.

"And you obviously care about other people," he said. "You're here because of what I did to your friend, not anything I did to you. So let me sweeten the deal. Your mommy and daddy will be in beds right next to you. The three of you can stare at the ceiling together."

"Okay," I said. "Yes. I'll do it."

"Do what?"

"Not say anything."

"To anybody. You will not say a goddamn word to anybody."

"Right. Yes. Nobody."

"I believe you," he said. "*Now.* The problem is that after you walk out of here, you won't be feeling the same level of terror that you are now. You'll relax. You'll feel safe again. You'll start to think that maybe I was bluffing."

"No, I won't."

Mr. Martin gently tapped the barrel of the gun against my forehead. "Again, I believe you now. But I need you to remember how scared you are. I need you to remember that you looked into my eyes and saw how deadly serious I was. You know that trick where you tie a string around your finger to help you remember something?"

"Uh-huh." I'd never done that, and didn't know anybody who had—it seemed kind of stupid—but I was familiar with the concept.

"We're going to do something like that. Give you a nice little reminder. I want you to stand up, and then you're going to very slowly walk into my kitchen, and if you give me even the slightest reason to believe that you're not taking my threat seriously, I will execute you. Understand?"

"I completely understand, yes."

Mr. Martin stood up and stepped away from me, giving me room to shakily get to my feet. My legs had gone numb and I worried that I might lose my balance and fall over.

"Go on," he said, waving the gun at me. "Nice and slow."

I walked into his kitchen, focusing all of my attention on trying to stay upright.

"Very good. You're doing great, Curtis. I'm proud of you. Walk over to the sink."

I did as I was told. I wasn't working out any kind of brilliant plan to escape or to somehow turn the tables back in my favor. I was going to do everything he said, slowly, and hope that he really intended to let me go.

"Open the drawer next to it. No, the other one. Yeah, that one."

I slid the drawer open. Silverware.

"Choose a knife."

I picked up a steak knife and held it up.

"That one? Eh, that's fine, I guess." Mr. Martin kept the gun pointed at me and took a step back, removing any possibility that I could charge at him with the knife before he could shoot me. "You're going to cut yourself. Don't worry, I didn't say *stab* yourself, just a cut. It'll hurt and it'll bleed but you won't die. Somewhere nobody will see."

"We don't need to—"

"Calm down. I'm not going to make you cut your dick. A guy like you doesn't walk around without a shirt, does he? Maybe a nice quick slice underneath some of that belly fat. Deep enough that it really stings. And later, when I'm not pointing this gun at you, you'll have a painful reminder of how scared you were."

I lowered the knife. "This is a bad idea."

"Well, yeah, the person who's about to cut himself usually doesn't think it's the best idea in the world."

"I get what you're trying to do. But I'm a bleeder. My blood is too thin, so it takes a long time for me to stop bleeding." This wasn't true, but there was a kid in school who had that problem. Hemophilia. When he got a bloody nose, he had to spend the rest of the day in the nurse's office. "If I have to keep changing the bandage, my parents might find out. Where am I supposed to keep hiding bloody bandages? What if it soaks through? I promised I won't say anything, and you're trying to make it harder for me to keep that promise."

Mr. Martin stared at me for an uncomfortably long moment. Then he nodded.

"Fair point," he said. "Put the knife back."

I'm pretty sure that a large part of his motivation was that he simply wanted to watch me cut myself. But I was relieved that he could see reason. I put the knife back in the drawer.

"I just want to say that I admire how brave you're being about this," Mr. Martin informed me. "No bawling or blubbering or anything to make me just want to shoot you. I can see why you were friends with Todd. He was brave...for as long as could reasonably be expected."

I said nothing.

"I'm going to let you go now," said Mr. Martin. "And we'll never speak of this again. If I get arrested, even if it's not your fault, I won't be able to make the call to keep you and your parents in one piece. If I find out that anybody knows details that I shared with you in confidence, it's a feeding tube for you. Got it?"

"Yes."

"Shake on it."

"Wait."

"What?"

"Will there be anybody else?" I asked.

Mr. Martin chewed on his lower lip for a moment. "No. I couldn't ask you to stay quiet if there were. I can control this, so I'm telling you, man to man, before we shake on it, that there will be no more victims. Deal?"

"Deal."

He stepped over to me, switched the gun from his right hand to his left, and then extended his right hand. I shook it. He had a painfully tight grip.

We silently walked out of the kitchen into the living room, and then over to the front door.

"Don't break our truce," he said.

"I won't."

He opened the door for me, and I stepped outside. After he closed the door, I resisted the urge to break into a sprint. I simply walked away from his house at a normal pace.

I wanted to scream. I wanted to cry. I wanted to punch things.

I'd completely failed.

Not just that—I'd made things *worse*. I'd gone from not being able to prove that Gerald Martin had abducted Todd to desperately needing for nobody else to prove it, either. Utter and total failure. I'd let down my best friend.

All I'd had to do was pull the trigger. I didn't have to murder him. Just shoot him in the leg. Or the gut. He would've fallen down.

There would have been a lot of explaining to do, but eventually I would've been a hero. Todd's parents would experience the devastation of extinguishing the last bit of hope that their son was alive, but at least they'd have closure. They could figure out how to move on. Now they'd never know the truth. They'd have to gradually come to accept that Todd was never returning home, yet have this lingering doubt that would last for the rest of their lives.

Squeeze the trigger. That's all I'd had to do. I had the son of a bitch at gunpoint.

I felt a dizzy spell coming on, so I stopped walking for a moment until it passed.

It came back as soon as I started walking again. I sat down on the sidewalk, closed my eyes, and tried not to throw up.

I couldn't sit here very long. It would be suspicious for some kid to just be sitting right there in the middle of the sidewalk, and I now had to do everything I could to not seem suspicious. I wished that I thought Mr. Martin was making up the whole thing about his unsavory friend, but I completely believed him. That friend was real.

I got back up and continued walking home, filled with anger and self-loathing and regret and pretty much every negative emotion I could summon. Hell, from a purely practical standpoint, I still had to repay the money I'd stolen from Dad's safe. I'd have to mow lawns like crazy to pay for a gun that I'd been too much of a chickenshit to fire. And my parents couldn't *know* that I was mowing all of these extra lawns, or doing whatever work I could get paid for, because they'd wonder where the money went, so I'd have to secretly work my ass off while maintaining my secret identity as a lazy bum. It would've been worth it if I could've brought Todd's killer to justice. It sure wasn't worth it now.

To keep myself sane, I needed to focus on the positive. I'd gotten out of there alive. Right now I could be dead or, more likely, several minutes into my slow death. There could be duct tape over my mouth and a thin blade carefully working its way around my eyeball socket. I could see staring into Mr. Martin's grinning, leering face with my good eye, begging him not to kill me, knowing that my muffled words wouldn't change his mind.

So, yeah, I was still alive.

That was something.

I'd monumentally fucked this up, but I'd also played it well enough for him to let me go. The note to my parents had served its purpose. Good planning there. And I'd successfully talked him out of making me cut myself. And, while I was praising myself, I should note that I'd pulled the gun out of my backpack before he could—

Shit.

I'd left my backpack there.

Goddamn it.

There wasn't anything irreplaceable in there. A few books. Just random stuff that I could put in there so that if he asked to peek inside, he wouldn't immediately see the gun. But I didn't own another backpack, and now I'd have to hope that my parents didn't notice that I'd lost it.

I sure as hell wasn't going back for it. For all I knew, Mr. Martin was kicking himself for letting me go. I wasn't going to deliver myself to his front door.

It had a tag that said, "*If found, please return to Curtis Black*" with my address, which was mildly concerning but nothing he couldn't easily find out on his own. Our name and address were in the phone book. It wasn't like my parents were worried about serial killers finding us.

Okay, so, I'd done a couple of things right, but I was also stupid enough to forget my backpack. My attempt to build up my self-esteem had, like this entire plan, been a dismal failure.

At least I didn't have any more dizzy spells as I walked out of Mr. Martin's neighborhood and into my own. I'd go home, rip up the note, take a really long nap, and then try to forget that this had ever happened. I couldn't let my parents suspect that anything was wrong, because if they pushed me too hard, I was liable to just start sobbing. Sure, ever since Todd disappeared it wasn't uncommon for me to have an emotional reaction out of nowhere, but now I had to be conscious of the truth versus the lie. I was having a meltdown because Todd was *still missing*, not because he'd been *murdered*.

The thought of police protection did occur to me. Tell them everything, especially about the man who would be on his way to mutilate us. He couldn't get at us if we were being closely watched by the authorities, could he?

Maybe.

And they wouldn't have a patrol car parked outside of our house forever. What were we going to do, go into a witness protection program? Change our identities? Did they even do that in real life, or was that just something I'd seen in movies?

Better to simply stick to the terms of our agreement, and pray that Mr. Martin did the same.

I was sweating again—or, more likely, I'd never stopped—as I turned onto my own street. I had my plan. Go home. Destroy the note. Sleep. Wake up and behave normally. Simple enough.

Then I saw my mother's car parked in our driveway.

8

I normally wasn't a very fast runner, but I could have qualified for the Olympics with how quickly I sprinted to my house. What the hell was my mom doing home? She *never* came home like this! If I were the kind of son to throw massive parties as soon as his parents left—which, alas, I was not—I'd never have been caught because my parents never surprised me with an early arrival like this. Never.

Had she forgotten something? Was she sick? Had she been fired? *Why was her car there?*

Okay, maybe this wasn't so bad. Maybe she hadn't looked on the dining room table yet. If she'd forgotten something, she might have just gone straight to retrieve it without a side trip to the dining room. If she was sick, maybe she'd gone right up to bed. If she'd been fired, maybe her vision was too blurry from crying to see the note I'd left on the table. Yes, I'd have to make up a story about why I hadn't been home, but I could handle that, I'd think of something in the next few moments, this might be all right, it might be fine, it might be okay, shit, shit, shit!

I ran up to the front door. It wouldn't be smart for me to fling open the door and burst inside the house, gasping for breath, so I decided to waste a few valuable moments just standing there, regaining my composure. I wiped the sweat off my face as best I could, then opened the door.

"Curtis?" my mom called out.

"Yeah, it's me!" I said.

I walked through the foyer into the living room. My mom was seated on the couch, holding the phone receiver to her ear. My note was on her lap.

"Never mind," she said to whomever she was speaking to. "He just came home. Yes, thank you for your help. Goodbye."

She hung up the phone, not quite slamming it down, but also not gently placing the receiver back in its cradle. She held up the note and waved it at me. "What the hell is this?"

"Hell" was the strongest curse word in my mother's vocabulary, and she used it sparingly, for maximum impact. My dad swore all the time, though he didn't go further than the s-word. I'd never heard him utter the f-word or any of the truly crass terms, as if he were obligated to report to the Standards & Practices department of a basic cable station.

That question, "What the hell is this?" conveyed an emotional combination that was seventy-five percent anger, twenty percent concern, and five percent relief. In the seconds after I said, "Yeah, it's me!" she was probably at one hundred percent relief, but upon seeing that I was home and safe, relief quickly slid down the scale and anger took its place.

Now I had to figure out what to say.

I was going to lie. That much was certain. Should I pretend it was a joke? She'd never believe that. I was a smart-ass but mean-spirited pranks weren't my thing. There was only one credible way to explain this.

"It's a note," I said.

That was not my plan. That was a delaying tactic while I tried to figure out how best to phrase what I needed to say.

Mom stood up. I was taller than her now, but it sure didn't feel like it at the moment. She had long brown hair that was completely straight—not a hint of a curl or frizz to be found. She was somebody who ate right, exercised regularly, but fourteen years later had never quite been able to reclaim her pre-Curtis body. Though it had been a long time since she'd been a physical threat to me, having her angrily get up off the couch was an intimidating sight…and I'd just spent some time with a serial killer.

She read the note out loud. "*Dear Mom & Dad. As you know, I am absolutely positive that Gerald Martin is guilty, and I have gone to his house to confront him. If you found this note, it means that I did not come back. Call the police and tell them everything. I love you. Curtis.*"

"Yeah," I said. I'm not sure what "yeah" was meant to convey.

"Did you go?"

I shook my head. "I was walking over there, but the second I saw his house I changed my mind. It was a stupid idea."

"You've got that right."

"So I came back home. I don't know what I was thinking. I'm sorry. It'll never happen again."

Mom gaped at me as if she'd come home to a burning house and my reaction had been, "*Sorry about the inferno; I'll never play with matches again.*"

"This is a big deal, Curtis," she said. "You're positive that he abducted Todd, so you went over there, alone? How would an idea like that even cross your mind? What did you think you were going to accomplish? How did you think it was going to turn out?"

I shrugged.

"Don't shrug at me. You're not six. Answer my question. How did you think it was going to turn out?'

"I said I don't know what I was thinking! I don't know how I thought it would turn out! It was a huge mistake, and I realized it as soon as I got there, so I turned around and came right back home. I messed up. I'm sorry I scared you."

"You're sorry." A dubious statement, not a question.

"Yes."

"You could have been killed."

"I know."

"I get that you're angry about what happened. I completely understand. I'm angry too. But you left us a note because you thought you might never come back. Do you get how *insane* that is?"

"Let me explain that part," I said. "I didn't leave that note because I thought I was never coming back. I left it so that I could tell *him* that I left it, so that he'd have to let me go. It wasn't supposed to be a goodbye note. It was my backup plan."

My mom's facial expression did not say *Oh, such a clever young lad you are to have had a backup plan!*

She didn't say anything, so I continued babbling. "If he took me hostage or whatever, I'd just say that I'd left you this note, and that you'd be calling the cops and sending them over to his house. Then he'd have no choice but to set me free. I was careful about this whole thing."

"What if he didn't believe you?" Mom asked.

"That would be a problem," I admitted.

"What if he decided that if he let you go, you'd go straight to the police, so he might as well kill you anyway?"

"I don't know."

"Do you get why I'm upset?"

"Yeah." Would she be less upset if she knew that I'd gone over there with a gun in my backpack? Probably not.

"And you get that I'm mad because I love you, right? I can't even describe how scared I was when I read that note. You're lucky I didn't have a heart attack before I called 911."

I wanted to ask just how much she'd told the 911 operator, but decided that it would be suspicious if I pressed her for that information right now.

Mom extended her arms. I stepped over there and gave her a tight hug.

That had been awful, and I felt incredibly guilty for giving her that great big scare, but at least I'd gotten through it.

"I think you need to see a psychiatrist," she told me.

We broke the hug.

"Nah," I said. "I'm fine."

"I didn't say that right. I said 'I think you need to see a psychiatrist' but I meant 'You're going to see a psychiatrist.' I'm going to start making calls today."

"Why?"

"Did you seriously just ask me why?"

"I'm totally fine," I assured her. "I made a big mistake, but I didn't go through with it, and I said it'll never happen again."

"You lost your best friend. It's normal to be sad, even depressed. The nightmares are normal. But—"

"I don't have nightmares."

"Yes, you do. I hear you talking in your sleep."

Did she? That was new information.

"This is all normal," Mom said. "But what is *not* normal is marching off, by yourself, to confront the man you think murdered Todd. I don't care if you changed your mind. The fact that you decided to do this, and planned it out carefully enough to leave your dad and I a note, makes me think that you really need to talk to somebody about how you're feeling."

"I'll talk to you about how I'm feeling."

"I mean an expert."

"I don't want to see a shrink."

"There's no shame in it."

"I wasn't very popular before. Now you not only want me to go back to school without my closest friend, but while I'm in therapy? I will literally be the least popular kid in the entire school. Nobody will want to be seen with me. I'll never have a girlfriend. I'll have to live with you for the rest of my life. Do you really want me living with you when I'm eighty?"

Mom raised an eyebrow. "I can't tell if you're trying to be funny or melodramatic."

"Both. Please, don't make me see a shrink. Give me one more chance."

"This isn't punishment, Curtis. That part is coming in a minute. This is something that I think might really help you work through this. You don't have to publicize it. They don't sell T-shirts that you wear to show that you're a customer. Nobody has to know, and you need to talk to somebody who has experience with this sort of thing."

I really did not want to talk to a psychiatrist. But I was trying to make this whole conversation finally come to an end, and if I kept protesting, it would drag on forever, or until she cut it short with the dreaded "We'll discuss it when your father gets home." I decided to let her sort-of win this one. "I'll think about it."

"I'm not saying you have to see a psychiatrist every week for the rest of your life. I'd like you to go once. If you hate it, you don't have to go back, but I'm going to ask you to go one time with an open mind. Will you do that for me?"

What was I supposed to say to that? She thought I was

completely deranged, and the truth was even worse than what she knew! If she found out that not only had I actually gone through with my idiotic plan, but that I'd brought along a gun, and actually pointed the gun at Mr. Martin, she'd probably have me committed to an asylum. One of those poorly lit ones, where you walked down the hallway hearing the echoes of patients' maniacal laughter, where straitjackets were the official attire.

"Yeah," I said. "I'll do it at least once."

She gave me another hug.

"I love you, Curtis," she said. "I just don't want to see anything bad happen to you."

"I love you, too."

"And now, punishment."

Dammit.

She broke the hug and stepped away. I hoped this would be one of those fake-out punishments, where she'd smile and say "Your punishment is that you have to give your mother a kiss!" or something cute and amusing like that.

"You're grounded until school starts again," she informed me. "Think of it as house arrest."

"What's house arrest?" I asked.

"It's something they've started doing. Instead of going to jail, criminals can't leave their house. There's some kind of monitoring equipment. You won't have the monitoring equipment, and you can go out into the yard to get some exercise, but I expect you to be close enough to hear the phone ring. Because I will call and check up on you, and if you don't answer, we will repeat this conversation but it won't be anywhere near as enjoyable. Got it?"

"What about mowing lawns?" I asked.

"You haven't done that since Todd went missing."

"I thought I might start again."

"Do you even have any customers left? Wouldn't they all have found somebody else to do it?"

"Maybe."

Mom sighed, like I was trying to exploit a loophole in my punishment. "If you want to earn some money, I'll allow that, but you have to give me their name and phone number. And if you think I won't bother to call them to check up on you, you are very sorely mistaken."

"Okay."

"Consider yourself lucky. If I waited to discuss this with your father, your punishment would've been worse."

"I'm glad you took the initiative."

Mom glanced at her wristwatch. "And now I'm going to get in trouble. I said I was just running straight home and back. I forgot my purse."

She gave me one more hug, grabbed her purse, and left.

Now I could properly react to the events of the day, which I did by hurrying into the bathroom, crouching down beside the toilet, and vomiting until there was nothing left to purge.

I flushed the toilet but continued to sit on the bathroom floor for a while.

How bad was my situation, really? I didn't much care that I was grounded. And maybe talking to a shrink would do me some good. He might have some useful insight on navigating the tricky social situation of maintaining a truce with a serial killer.

Mr. Martin wouldn't be punished for Todd's death, but I wasn't some knight in the Middle Ages who'd sworn an oath to avenge the king. I was a teenager. It wasn't my responsibility to see the bad guy brought to justice. I hadn't been some trembling little kid who was too frightened to tell the authorities what he saw—I'd shared every detail about that night, and it wasn't my fault that they didn't have enough information to hang him for it.

My official level of peril came down to whether or not I could trust Mr. Martin to keep his end of the deal. He'd promised there would be no more victims. Would he stick to that?

Would he decide that I was a loose end that needed to be cut off? If I was wondering if he could be trusted, maybe he was wondering the same thing, and if he decided that I *couldn't* be...

Hard to believe that I'd thought this day would end with Mr. Martin being handcuffed and shoved into the back of a patrol car, while reporters gathered around me to hear the tale of the brave boy hero who'd ended the string of Alaska abductions.

Of course, right now I could also be standing in Mr. Martin's living room, staring at his bloody corpse, hearing sirens blaring in the distance as I desperately tried to find and get rid of every bit of evidence that I'd been there. I'd flee through his back door, praying there were no witnesses, and then I'd replay the events over and over and over and over in my mind, wondering if I'd missed something. And when there was a loud knock at the door and voices ordering me to open up immediately, I'd know that yes, I had indeed missed something, and hopefully my parents could afford a lawyer who was good enough to keep me from being tried as an adult. If Mr. Martin stuck to the truce, things were okay.

Until he gave me reason to believe otherwise, I'd assume that he was going to keep his word. Yes, if I waited until I had a reason, it might be too late, but it wasn't as if I had a wide array of options right now.

That was my plan. Wait and see.

Maybe Mr. Martin would flee the country.

My mom called about two hours later to check up on me. Then she called five minutes after that, just in case I'd thought her calls would happen in a predictable timeframe. I spent the day trying and failing to accomplish simple tasks like reading a book or paying attention to a TV show.

When my mom got home, she didn't say anything about our talk this morning. And she didn't pull my dad aside for a private conversation when he got home, so I wasn't sure if she'd decided he didn't need to know about my blunder, or if the time simply wasn't right.

After the dinner that my mom cooked, she cleared the table and started doing the dishes, because though times were changing, this particular gender role remained firmly in place in my house in 1979. My dad sat on the couch to watch television. He patted the cushion next to him to encourage me to join him.

At the commercial, he turned to me. "We need to talk."

This wasn't a surprise. Mom must have called him at work. "Okay."

"Have you been in my safe?"

9

peak, goddamn it, speak! my brain screamed at me as I just kind of sat there with an unintelligent expression on my face. I needed to say something like, "Goodness, dear father, where would you get such an absurd idea? Me, disrespecting your privacy and committing vile acts of thievery? Never! Why, I take offense at the very idea! I challenge thee to a duel!"

What I said was a mix of "Huh?" and "What?" If it had come out as "Whuh?" that would've been bad enough, but I actually said "Hut?" which made no sense. I'm pretty sure that a thick sheen of perspiration instantly materialized on my forehead, with the word "Guilty" magically appearing in the way the light reflected off the moisture.

"Have you been in my safe?" he repeated.

Stay calm. Maintain eye contact. Look innocent.

"No, why?"

"Some money is missing from it."

"Are you kidding?"

My father liked puns and knock-knock jokes. He'd sometimes

make up knock-knock jokes on the spot, with varying degrees of success, and his puns often required so much explanation afterward that the humor was unable to make the full journey. What he did *not* do is falsely accuse his son of getting into his safe in an attempt to be amusing.

"I'm not kidding," he said. "Three hundred and fifty dollars is gone."

I couldn't believe this. He actually counted his money. How often did he count it? Weekly? Was it a creepy ritual that he performed every night before bed? I had a mental image of him as a greedy and miserly Scrooge McDuck, going through his precious stacks of cash one bill at a time to ensure that each and every one of them were accounted for. This was an inaccurate mental image, of course, since Scrooge McDuck was known for joyously diving into huge piles of money. Ebenezer Scrooge would have been a better comparison. I wasn't really into Dickens at the time.

Much later, reflecting upon this moment, it would occur to me that Dad almost certainly had *not* been counting his money as part of some obsessive-compulsive ritual, but rather that I'd left behind some sort of evidence that I'd been in the safe. A smudge on the combination dial or something. I wasn't exactly a master criminal. But at the time, my only explanation was the Scrooge McDuck one.

"Well, it wasn't me," I said. "Do you think somebody broke in?"

"No."

"Did you ask Mom about it?"

"Of course I asked your mother about it." Dad was not a fan of dumb questions, especially those that implied that he was so careless as to not bother asking my mother—who also had the combination to the safe and would be entitled to its contents—about the missing cash before confronting their child.

"Oh. I don't know what to tell you."

"Hmmm." My father was able to convey a lot with "Hmmm."

In this case, it meant: *I don't believe you for a second, but I'm not going to push the issue...for now.*

I had to lie. What else was I going to do? Confess to buying a gun from some sleazy guy in a van? Being forced to see a psychiatrist would be the least of my worries. I could say that I stole it to buy myself something else, which would at least keep the "unregistered gun" element out of the discussion, but then I'd have to produce the item. Though my parents couldn't account for everything randomly strewn around my room—nor could I—there was nothing that I could present as an illicit three-hundred-and-fifty-dollar purchase.

Should I say that I stole the money to pay for some hookers? Nah.

The only good move here was to continue to lie my ass off. He knew I'd taken the money but he couldn't prove it beyond all reasonable doubt. Unlike a criminal case, I could be convicted and punished without a trial. "We know damn well you did it," was sufficient.

For now, it appeared that he was going to leave it at "Hmmm."

I REALLY WANTED to go to bed early, but that would be suspicious, and I had to behave with maximum normality. So I waited for Mom and Dad to go to bed before I went to bed myself, where I slept like crap. My previous night's sleep, when I lay there thinking that the gun under my bed might go off and shoot me through the mattress, was like slumbering on a fluffy cloud as angels played lullabies on their harps. I just stared at the ceiling, feeling absolutely miserable.

WHEN I WAS ELEVEN, I found a dirty magazine in the woods.

I don't remember which one it was. It wasn't *Playboy* or *Penthouse*—it had a "just the pictures" format, aimed at an audience that didn't even seek the illusion of reading it for the articles. It was just page after page of glossy pictures of nekkid ladies, featuring the down-there grooming standards of the time.

Many of these "And that's when I became a horndog!" origin stories begin with finding a magazine in the woods. I'm not sure how they get out there. Perhaps there's a pornography fairy who hides them for pre-pubescent boys to discover. You never hear, for example, about middle-aged women finding an issue of *Hustler* in the woods while going for a hike.

This magazine became my most treasured possession. I showed it to Todd, of course, who calmly flipped through the pages while politely nodding his head in approval at the fine visuals. I showed it to various other kids around the neighborhood, swearing them to secrecy, and they were all suitably impressed. Requests to borrow it were denied.

Then I showed it to my friend Markus, who was my age (though we'd never shared a teacher) and lived at the end of the block. He looked through the entire magazine, not missing a page, and then informed me that he was going to tell my mom.

"You'd better not!" I told him, hoping that a savage beating was implied.

He didn't tell on me. Instead, he spent the next several weeks *threatening* to tell on me. Pretty much any time we were together he'd say "I'm gonna tell your mom about that magazine!"

To be clear, he wasn't blackmailing me. It wasn't like, "Hey, give me that popsicle or I'll tell your mom about the nudie mag!" There were no conditions placed upon me. Simply the ongoing warning that today might be the day that he knocked on my front door and had a serious conversation with my mother about how she was raising a pervert.

Clearly, he was getting off on the power he had over me. I was sick to my stomach with anxiety. Why squander his power by telling on me too soon, when he could stretch it out, enjoy my misery? It was awful. I'm not saying that my every waking moment was a living hell, but there was a mild awareness of the situation that never *quite* receded completely into the background of my mind. I'd be sitting at home watching television and suddenly "He's gonna tell my mom about the magazine!" would pop into my mind, and I'd want to throw up.

Eventually, instead of telling my mom, he told *his* mom. She looked at me like I was the Gulfstream Acres Rapist and did the "Either you can tell your mom or I can" thing. So I went home, presented the magazine—which, yes, I had kept all this time—and confessed to being a filthy little perv. Mom asked how long ago I'd found it, and despite the temptation to say, "Why, just now! I brought it to your attention immediately!" I told the truth, just in case there was follow-up from Markus or his mother.

At the time of my confession, we conveniently had a fire going in the fireplace. So my mom made me toss the magazine into the flames. I was a little heartbroken as I watched the pages, upon which I had gazed so very many times, curl up, blacken, and turn to ash, but there was also intense relief.

It was over.

I no longer had this hanging over my head. Markus' power was gone.

I had my life back.

That experience had been absolutely miserable...and what had been at stake? Some embarrassment. Maybe a lecture about respecting women. Possibly a sooner-than-I-wanted discussion of the birds and the bees. (My father sat me down for The Talk two years later, which I now present in its entirety: "You know all that stuff, right?" "Yeah." "Okay, good.")

That secret was about a magazine. This was about a serial killer.

That little secret gnawed away at me for a few weeks. What would this one be like? Steel shark jaws? Would I ever be able to *not* think about it? How could I make it through any day without this consuming my every waking thought? Would I ever hit a point where it simply didn't matter anymore, or was this my life now? Nothing but stomach-churning anxiety?

I could almost imagine Mr. Martin with a knife to my throat, while I thought, *well, at least my suffering is over.*

Mom hadn't mentioned the psychiatrist to me again, but it definitely wasn't forgotten. She'd just say "C'mon, let's go," when it was time for my appointment.

I fell asleep at some point, I suppose, because I opened my eyes when I heard my parents moving around, getting ready for work. I closed them again when I heard my doorknob turn, and I pretended to be asleep as somebody quietly opened my door, waited for a moment, then closed it again. They weren't in the habit on peeking in on me before they left for the day, but obviously things had changed.

After they left, I got up. Considered brushing my teeth but decided there was no rush. Had a bowl of cereal with milk that tasted sour even though it was from a brand-new carton. Watched some television, by which I mean I sat in the living room looking vaguely in the direction of the television.

I glanced over at the clock. It was almost noon.

The phone rang.

Actually, the first ring is what caused me to glance at the clock, but I hadn't immediately recognized the sound as having come from the telephone. I assumed it was Mom. Since this was the olden days before caller ID, I had to answer the call to find out who was on the other end.

"Hello?"

"Curtis?" It wasn't Mom.

"Mr. Martin?"

"Check outside your front door," he said. There was a rustling that sounded like wind blowing against the mouthpiece. He must've been calling from an outdoor pay phone.

He hung up.

I did not want to check outside my front door.

Okay, he couldn't simultaneously call me and stand out there waiting to murder me. The idea that he might've booby trapped the door flashed through my mind, but I decided that was ridiculous. The door was not going to explode when I opened it.

I opened up the living room curtains and peeked through them. Nobody in our front yard. From this angle, I'd be able to see if somebody was standing there, but not if they'd set anything down in front of the door.

Despite having just decided that a booby-trapped door was ridiculous, I didn't want to open it. I'd go out through the back door, circle the house, and see what Mr. Martin was talking about.

Unless that was his plan. Fool me into thinking that the front door was unsafe, when the *real* danger lurked out back.

Nope. Nope, nope, nope. I was getting paranoid. It was wise to be safe by going out the back door instead of the front, but I couldn't let myself descend into paranoid madness. Maintaining my sanity was going to be difficult enough without making it worse for myself.

I went out the back door.

Stealthily walked around the side of the house.

Peeked around the corner.

My backpack rested in front of the door.

I hurried over to it. A note was attached to it with a safety pin. "*Hi! Found this and wanted to return it! Good thing your address was on there! No reward necessary, just trying to be nice! Sincerely, a Good Samaritan!*"

Smart. The note wouldn't give anything away if somebody besides me had found the backpack first. I picked it up and went back inside through the non-booby-trapped front door.

I set my backpack on the coffee table. Had he tampered with it? Had he included any nasty surprises inside?

Mr. Martin could have easily said, "I left your backpack at your front door" instead of "Check outside your front door." He wanted to create that moment of anxiety and uncertainty.

I stared at my backpack for a while. Longer than a sane person would stare at his backpack.

The backpack had to be fine. There wasn't a venomous snake coiled inside. If I died under mysterious circumstances, like an exploding backpack, it might come right back to him. If he wanted to assassinate me, this isn't the way he'd go about it.

Right?

That sounded right.

Not that I was in any way an expert on the inner workings of the mind of a serial killer. Maybe I was looking for logic where it didn't exist.

He'd done me a favor. School was about to start soon, and now I didn't have to explain to my parents why I needed a new backpack. He didn't want me to have to tell lies any more than necessary. Returning my backpack made complete sense.

I unzipped it very slowly.

No cobra lashed out at me.

I unzipped it all the way and peeked inside. It looked okay.

Finally I worked up the courage and rifled through the contents. Everything was there. Apart from the gun, the backpack and its contents were no different than they had been when I walked into his house.

I took my backpack to my room. One less thing to worry about.

The phone rang about half an hour later. It was Mom, checking up on me. She called three more times, but Mr. Martin didn't call again.

I skipped lunch. Had to force myself to eat dinner.

Slept horribly.

The next day I skipped lunch *and* breakfast. Dinner was chicken pot pies, which I loved, though I still had to struggle to get down the last few bites. Mom didn't bring up the psychiatrist and Dad didn't bring up the safe, but I knew that neither of those subjects would stay buried for long.

Slept horribly again.

Woke up angry.

I'd been mad at myself, but now all of my anger was directed at Mr. Martin. He'd murdered Todd. He'd murdered at least two other kids in Fairbanks, and possibly a couple more elsewhere. He'd turned my life into nothing but twenty-four hours a day of dread.

Well, fuck him.

I wasn't going to keep playing his game.

10

To be clear, the details of *how* I was going to stop playing his game still eluded me. Unless it was bullshit, he still had the guy who'd mutilate everybody in my household if Mr. Martin got arrested. Honestly, Mr. Martin had been right: now that I wasn't in immediate danger, his threat did feel more like a bluff.

Not enough of a bluff to make me run to the authorities, though.

I needed a really good plan. Something much better than "Go over there with a gun and try to make him incriminate himself." I needed something ingenious. "Ingenious," sadly, was not a word used to describe me, unless there was sarcasm involved.

As expected, the visit to the psychiatrist happened without notice—pretty much "Get in the car and let's go." Unlike my own anger, my mom's had faded, and on the drive over she assured me that this was something that might help me figure some things out, and that if I didn't like it she wouldn't force me to go back, but that she wanted me to at least give it the full hour. I promised that I would.

The shrink, Dr. Wasser, looked exactly like I envisioned a psychiatrist, since I envisioned them as men with ponytails and goatees, dressed entirely in black, leaving at the end of the day to recite poetry at a coffee bar. He looked about sixty years old, but of course I was only fourteen, and he might have been ten or fifteen years younger than that.

I lay down on his couch, and he licked the end of his pencil before opening his notebook.

He spoke in a soothing tone that I'm pretty sure he practiced. I didn't want to be here, but I was willing to accept the possibility that this might help, so I decided that I was going to tell the truth about everything except my time in Mr. Martin's house. As far as I knew, he wasn't allowed to blab about anything I told him, even to my mother, but to play it safe I decided that the parameters of truth were the same ones I was using with my parents.

It was actually fairly similar to the line of questioning I'd experienced with the state troopers, except that Mr. Wasser kept asking how I felt about it, whereas the state troopers were not particularly concerned with that part of the story. I was honest. I felt scared. Angry. Helpless. He nodded a lot and kept writing in his notebook.

I honestly didn't realize how much talking I was doing until he informed me that it was the end of my session, and I hadn't yet had to lie about anything. "Hopefully I'll see you again next week," he said.

"Yeah, okay."

On the drive home, Mom asked me how it went. I thought it would be funny to tell her that he said I had an Oedipal complex, but my mom and I didn't really have the kind of relationship where I told jokes like that. So I just told her it had been fine. She asked if

I'd be willing to go back next week, and I said yeah. She seemed extremely happy to hear this and didn't push me for further details about the session.

I was much hungrier at dinner time, even though meatloaf wasn't one of my favorites (my mom used way too much ketchup). I'm not suggesting for one second that I felt *good* about life in general, but I'd managed to hold back the sense of despair.

As we were finishing up, there was a knock at the door.

Dad, whose hatred of being interrupted at dinner time was something he should probably speak to a psychiatrist about, scowled, pushed back his chair, and went to answer it.

"Hi, I hope we didn't bother you," I heard from the foyer. It sounded like Todd's dad, who had never come over to my house before.

"No, no, not at all, come in," said Dad, whose rage about being interrupted during his meal did not extend to grieving parents.

Mom and I got up from the table as Dad came into the living room with Todd's parents. They both looked like they'd been crying, though Todd's dad had done a better job of drying his eyes.

"We apologize for interrupting you," said Todd's dad. "We just came over to say goodbye."

"Goodbye?" I asked.

"We're moving." He gestured to his wife. "We're going to stay with her sister in Oregon for a while until we figure out what to do next."

"It's been really hard, as I'm sure you can imagine," said Todd's mom, her voice trembling. "We've tried to get through it the best we can, but with school starting next week...it's too much. We haven't given up hope; we just need a new environment."

I could see in Todd's father's face that he *had* given up hope. He knew his son was dead. He knew Todd wasn't going to return home and wonder why a different family was living in his house.

I desperately wished I could give his mom that same level of closure.

"Thank you for what you did," Todd's dad told me. "You were always a good friend to him. You did everything you could, and we'll never forget it."

I didn't know what to say to that. Mostly I just wanted to start crying, but I held it together.

"If you need anything, please don't hesitate to let us know," said Mom.

The five of us stood in the living room, ill at ease, until finally Todd's dad said, "Well, we'd better get back. We've got a lot of packing left to do."

Nobody seemed sure if this was a hugging moment or not. They knew each other as "my son's friend's parents" but had never been friends themselves. Finally, Todd's mom decided that it was indeed such a moment. Hugs were exchanged all around, and then they left.

I STOOD in the shower and decided that though I couldn't let Mr. Martin get away with his crimes, there was no rush.

As long as he stuck to the truce, I had time. Todd was dead. There was nothing I could do for him. He and the others weren't going to come back to life. I liked to believe that I was seeking justice instead of revenge, but either way, I thought the "dish served cold" saying was appropriate. I'd nail that son of a bitch in due time.

By waiting, I'd gain more of an advantage. His advantage over me was that the authorities couldn't protect my family and I forever. If I ratted Mr. Martin out, I'm sure there'd be a state trooper parked outside of our home for a while, but they weren't going to assign us twenty-four-hour protection forever. Eventually, and probably fairly soon, Mr. Martin's friend would have his opportunity.

But this worked the other way, too. Was his plan to call his friend once a day for the rest of his life? Surely there would be a point where he'd decide that he was safe, that the situation had blown over. Would the news of a child killer being arrested in Alaska make its way down to the lower forty-eight? Just how closely was his friend—if this guy even existed—monitoring things up here? When Mr. Martin was given his phone call after being arrested, would he squander it on calling that guy?

I didn't know. All I knew was that the longer I waited, the greater the chance of taking him down. I wasn't talking about years. Whatever sickness in his mind made him commit these atrocities might become uncontrollable if I waited too long. But weeks? Months? Enough time for him to let down his guard.

For all I knew, he was having sleepless nights, too. Waking up in a cold sweat from a nightmare where the FBI broke down his door. Seeing steel bars everywhere he looked. Wondering if each day, each hour, each *minute*, could be his last moment of freedom.

I loved the idea of him suffering like this.

So, yeah, I'd wait.

AND THEN SCHOOL STARTED AGAIN.

Fairbanks had three different elementary schools, where you went from first through sixth grade. In seventh grade, everybody was together at Ryan Junior High, so your possible social group suddenly tripled in size. In ninth grade, everybody would be divided between two different high schools, so former friends would become fierce rivals.

So as I began eighth grade, there were a lot of unfamiliar faces walking the halls—seventh graders who'd gone to different elementary schools. And though I recognized pretty much all of the eighth graders from last year, only a third of them were kids I'd grown up with. I hadn't been particularly popular last year, mostly just hanging out with Todd. This meant that my new identity, as I walked into the school, was "the kid whose best friend is missing and probably dead."

Eighth graders are not very good at expressing sympathy for this sort of thing. My presence in the school was awkward and strange. Lots of stares and whispers. I'm not saying that the crowds parted as I walked down the hallway, but there was a definite sense—possibly imagined on my part—that they felt like my tragedy might be contagious.

Todd and I weren't devoid of other friends, but while I'm not saying that our mutual friends tried to avoid me, I got the definite sense that they weren't comfortable talking to me. The usual, "Hey, how was your summer?" small talk didn't work anymore. They were his friend too, but it felt like all of the *weirdness* was on me. In fifth grade, my classmate Mark's mother had died, and before he returned to school, the teacher had given all of us a lecture about how we needed to be really nice to him. When he came back, we all just kind of stayed away from him, which in retrospect was horrifically cruel. I didn't actually make the Mark connection at the time, but I could tell that the other kids didn't much want to be around me, because if they were they might have to say something about Todd.

I had all-new teachers, who presumably hadn't been given a dossier on who was friends with the missing boy, so they didn't treat me any differently, at least.

This school year was going to suck.

When my mom asked how the first day went, I told her it had gone fine.

Maybe school would be okay after everybody had a chance to adjust, after my peers realized that I wasn't going to burst into tears at random times and scream, "Why, God, why?"

The entire week sucked, but Friday sucked less than Monday had, so, yes, it was entirely possible that eighth grade might eventually cease being completely miserable.

Friday at lunch, I sat in the cafeteria. I wasn't seated at a table by myself—there wasn't enough room for somebody to be a complete outcast—but I wasn't actually eating *with* anybody. A girl I didn't recognize sat down across from me.

She'd clearly chosen this seat on purpose, not just because it was the only open spot. She had thick glasses. Short brown hair. Freckles. Crooked front teeth, which I saw when she smiled as if in greeting.

"Hi," she said.

"Hi."

"Are you Curtis?"

"Yeah."

"Hi."

"Hi."

"I'm Tina."

"Hi, Tina."

She sat there, as if working up her nerve. "I just wanted to say that I'm sorry about what happened to your friend." She glanced down at her lap, then looked back up at me again. "And if there's anything I can do to help, don't hesitate to let me know."

"Thanks, Tina," I said. "That's really cool of you."

She nodded. "Thanks," she said back. She immediately grimaced, as if realizing that "Thanks" was the wrong thing to say. She reached up and adjusted her glasses. As she lowered her hand, I saw that she'd written on it in pen.

Had she given herself crib notes for our conversation?

She noticed that I'd seen her hand and immediately looked positively mortified. She looked like she wanted to say something, couldn't find the words, and then got up from the table, seemingly on the verge of tears. She hurried out of the cafeteria. I wanted to call out or go after her, but I thought that might draw everybody's attention to her and make things even worse.

I continued on with my day. One advantage to being a social outcast was that I wasn't tempted to talk during class, although of course by the eighth grade teachers had abandoned the "Write your name on the board if you're naughty" approach. Based on first-week impressions, I liked five of my seven teachers, which was a decent enough ratio.

When the final bell rang, I made a trip to my locker then headed outside. I scanned the crowd of junior high students for Tina. Thought I saw somebody who might be her, walking toward the furthest bus. I hurried after her, still not sure I had the right person.

"Tina?" I called out.

She stopped walking right before she got on the bus and turned around. I had the right person. She looked at me, looked at the ground, looked at me, looked at the bus, then looked at me again.

"Hi," she said. She stepped away from the bus so that we could talk without getting trampled.

I speed-walked over to her. "Hi."

"I'm not stupid," she informed me.

"I never said you were."

"I get nervous and sometimes my mind goes blank. I thought it was important to say something to you about your friend because I know how much it hurts to lose somebody, but I didn't want to just stare at you because my brain froze up. So I wrote a couple of words on my hand just in case. That's all."

"I totally get it."

Tina stepped toward the bus, then stepped back in front of me. "So that's what I was doing."

"I appreciate you coming over and talking to me," I said. "I was kind of feeling like I was being shunned."

Tina nodded. "My mom died a couple of years ago and that's how I felt. It's like people don't know what to say to you. Adults will say 'Oh, I'm so sorry,' but other kids act like they're spooked."

"Sorry about your mom."

"It's okay."

"How did she die?"

"I don't want to talk about it. Cancer, but I don't want to talk about it. Leukemia."

"I'm sorry."

"It's okay."

"Don't be embarrassed about writing notes on your hand," I told her. "One time we were playing dodgeball in gym class, and I had to pee, and when I got hit really hard I wet my pants, I mean *really* wet them. So the other kids were laughing at me, and I tried to say that I'd spilled a drink, even though I obviously didn't have a drink out there on the floor of the gymnasium while we were playing dodgeball. Then I started to cry. So I'd wet my pants, lied about it, and now was crying in front of everybody." Sharing this anecdote had felt like a good idea when I began, but halfway through I'd decided that this tale of pissing my pants, shared in the spirit of solidarity, was not going to impress her very much, but now that I'd started it I had to see it through to the shameful end.

"How long ago was that?" Tina asked.

"Third grade. But it still hurts. Unlike your hand. I'll have forgotten about your hand by the time I get home." I hoped she understood that I was specifically referencing the writing on her hands, and wasn't simply saying that she had unmemorable hands.

Tina smiled. Her crooked teeth were *endearingly* crooked.

I decided that I should ask her out on a date.

I'd never asked a girl out on a date.

But I'd also never faced off against a psychopathic serial killer until recently. If I could walk into Mr. Martin's living room with a gun, I could ask Tina out, right? Surely one of these things was way easier than the other.

"Do you want to go to the movies?" I asked.

Tina blinked in surprise. She glanced down at her hand, as if she might have written a note on it to explain what to say in response. "What's playing?"

The Goldstream Theater in 1979 had only two screens. One was playing *Alien,* which was rated R and which I'd heard was the goriest movie ever made (apparently the alien popped out of some guy's stomach and you saw every grisly detail) and the other was playing *Rocky II.* Tina didn't look like somebody who was into boxing movies. Maybe the movies weren't the best choice right now.

"Or we could go to the library," I said.

Or we could go to the library. That is what came out of my mouth. *Or we could go to the library.* I might as well have invited her to the Geek Festival of Nerdy Dorks. *Or we could go to the library.* Jesus Christ. I could now see the merit of taking notes on your hand.

"I love the library," said Tina.

"I mean the real library, not the school one," I said, in case she thought I was inviting her to the Ryan Junior High library for our first date.

"I'd have to ask my dad," she said.

"Okay."

"He's very over-protective. He might say no."

"Well, if he says no, we'll…I don't know. Something."

"I'll let you know what he said on Monday."

If she let me know on Monday, we'd be making plans for the

following weekend, which meant that there might be a non-R-rated, non-boxing movie playing. But I'd stick with the library idea, since she hadn't immediately pointed at me and let out a braying laugh.

We both stood there for a moment.

"I should get on my bus," Tina said.

"Yeah, yeah, me too. Nice meeting you."

"Nice meeting you." She smiled and got on her bus.

Holy shit. I'd asked a girl out, and she'd said yes (with a disclaimer). I hadn't seen that coming, after the way this week started.

I walked away from the bus and heard some snickers. I glanced over and saw Ed Loreen, bully supreme, standing with a couple of his sycophantic friends, Burt and Josh. Ed had gone to a different elementary school, so I hadn't made his acquaintance until last year. He was tall and about as muscular as a fourteen-year-old gets. I'd witnessed him picking on several other kids, but because we didn't share any classes, he'd generally left me alone.

"Did you just ask her out?" Ed asked.

"Yeah."

"I didn't know fat fucks like you were allowed to do that." He placed a cupped hand to his ear. "I think I hear her puking on the bus right now." Burt and Josh laughed hysterically. Ed mimed the way Tina was probably puking, and their laughter intensified.

I had been raised with the idea that a bully was only seeking attention, so the best thing you could do was ignore him. But, again, I'd faced off against Mr. Martin and not been decapitated.

If I could do that, and I could ask out a girl I'd just met, I could kick Ed Loreen's ass. Right now.

11

E d and his dipshit buddies looked confused as I walked over to them. They weren't used to this sort of thing.

In a perfect narrative, I would have laid him out with one punch, a solid haymaker to the jaw. As he lay on the ground, unmoving but probably not dead, the other students would have begun a slow clap that intensified until the entire school, faculty included, was cheering my victory.

In an alternate narrative, Ed would have punched me in the face as soon as I strode up to him. My legs would collapse beneath me, and I'd lay on the ground, tears of shame stinging my cheeks as I learned a harsh lesson about overconfidence.

What actually happened is that the fight played out like most fights do in real life: an embarrassing spectacle to behold. More of an awkward shoving match, with few punches thrown and none of them landing particularly well. Oh, everybody outside of the school immediately began watching, but we really weren't doing much to give the audience a good show. I said "You want some? Huh?" once and Ed said it twice. He scratched my arm and I accidentally stepped on his foot while we were bumbling around, but there wasn't much else in the way of injuries.

"Break it up! Break it up!" a teacher shouted, making his way through the crowd of kids who'd circled around us. He tugged Ed out of the way and the "fight" was over.

"Not even one week?" Principal Taylor asked. "You couldn't keep it together for one single week?"

"He called me a fat eff-blank-blank-blank," I said. We were alone in his office. Ed sat right outside, awaiting his turn in the hot seat.

"He called you a what?"

"A fat, you know."

"I don't know. That's why I asked."

I was not dumb enough to say, "A fat *fuck*, Principal Taylor! He called me a fat *fuck*!" "He used the F-word when he was calling me fat," I explained. That sounded very tattletale-ish. I wasn't trying to get Ed in trouble for his use of salty language; I was trying to justify why I'd attacked him.

"The F-word."

"You know what the F-word is, right?" I asked.

"Yes, Mr. Black, I do. Why did he call you that?"

I wasn't sure how to answer this. Because I was obese? This was long before anybody would wag their finger at you for "fat-shaming." Making fun of somebody's weight was considered totally within the bounds of fair play.

I didn't think I should say, "Because he's a dick."

I shrugged.

Principal Taylor rubbed his forehead as if suffering from an excruciating migraine. I didn't doubt that he had a headache, but the gesture did seem calculated to show me how much dismay I was bringing into his life. "I don't want to give anybody detention the first week. That starts things off on a bad note. I'm going to bring Ed in here, and you two are going to shake hands, and if you can do me that tiny little favor, we'll pretend this didn't happen."

"Thanks."

"Get up and open the door, will you?"

I stood up and opened the door. Principal Taylor called for Ed to come into his office. Ed walked through the doorway.

"I want you two to shake hands and apologize to each other," Principal Taylor said. "No further punishment. If I see either of you in my office again, it will be a very different outcome. Do you understand?"

"Sure," said Ed.

"So do it. Shake hands. Apologize."

Ed and I shook hands.

"Sorry," I said.

"Sorry," he said.

"Go home and enjoy your weekend," Principal Taylor told us. Ed and I left.

I walked ahead of him. I'd missed the bus, and the junior high was nowhere close to walking distance from home, so I'd have to call my mom at work and ask her to pick me up after the bank closed. It wasn't *too* far out of her way, so as long as I came up with a good excuse for why I'd missed the bus it wouldn't be a big deal.

My first real (if inept) fight and my first time asking out a girl, both on the same day. This was going to be a very interesting school year.

"Hey!" Ed called out to me.

I stopped walking and looked back at him.

"You tried to kick my ass," he said. "I respect that."

"Oh, uh, thanks." *You're welcome?* What was the proper response to this?

"We're not friends or anything like that, so don't go getting the wrong idea. But we're cool. You need anything, let me know."

"I will."

Ed walked past me. I watched him go, wondering how much weirder this day was going to get.

Instead of making up an excuse that might be analyzed for gaps in logic, I just called my mom and told her that I'd been talking to some other kids and didn't realize that the busses had left. Since the reason made me look like a dumbass, she'd believe it.

"How was school?" Mom asked, after I got in the car.

"Fine."

"Anything interesting happen?"

"Not really."

"Learn anything?"

"Eh."

"Do you have a favorite teacher yet?"

"Mrs. Davis."

"What does she teach?"

"English."

"Why's she your favorite?"

I started to say, "She's nice," but clearly Mom was fishing for something more substantial. I needed to throw her some sort of bone, even if it was a smart-assed bone. "She doesn't worship Satan."

"Okay."

"All of my other teachers are obviously Satanists," I explained. "They didn't actually sacrifice a goat during class, but if there'd been a goat in the classroom, they totally would've sacrificed it to the dark lord."

"Then it's good that there wasn't a goat in the classroom," said Mom.

"Right? I like Mrs. Davis because she doesn't make us scoot all of our desks out of the way to make room for the pentagram."

"Wise guy."

"WHAT ARE your plans for the weekend?" asked Dad.

"Mow some lawns," I said. If Tina's father gave his blessing for me to take out his sweet innocent daughter, I'd need some money. I wasn't going to tell Mom or Dad about it unless I got a "yes" answer. I didn't want them getting all excited and then needing to console me.

Dad nodded. "Yeah, you should probably try to earn some money." The way he said it, I could tell that the issue of the missing cash from his safe was still very much on his mind.

I didn't acknowledge the blatant accusation in his tone. "Yep."

"Mrs. Deckle is looking for somebody to help her assemble a shed. I'll call her, if you want."

I didn't want to assemble a shed. But I did need the pay, and I didn't want a lecture from my father on not being a lazy piece of crap. "Okay," I said.

"It'll be good exercise."

"I already said okay. You don't need to say that it'll make me less fat."

Dad blinked. My weight was not something I ever acknowledged in his presence. Nobody tried to pretend that I was svelte; we simply didn't discuss it.

"I'll call her right now," said Dad.

IT TOOK the entire weekend to put together the shed. Mrs. Deckle, an elderly woman with dead eyes, paid pauper wages and stopped the clock for bathroom breaks. Her lemonade had seeds floating in it and was so sour that I'm convinced this was her recipe:

Step One: Squeeze lemons into glass.

Step Two: Serve.

She was a cruel taskmaster. She barked orders at me the entire time, punctuating them with "Dammit!" if I didn't immediately understand what she was trying to say, which was most of the time. "Move it to your left! No, no, your other left! No, no, your *other* left, dammit!" I'm honestly surprised she didn't pick up one of the planks of wood and start beating me with it.

When I was taking an unpaid bathroom break, she pounded on the door. "What are you doing in there?" she demanded. "You'd better not be masturbating in my bathroom!"

I found it disturbing that she thought being berated by a mean old lady all day would make me so horny that I couldn't control myself. I was sore and exhausted and miserable and she was far from a visual treat. "I'm going number two!" I informed her.

"You save that kind of thing for your own house!"

Normally I would agree with her. As a guest in somebody's home for a short visit, bathroom visits should be quick and efficient. But these were sixteen-hour days, starting so early that my bodily functions hadn't yet kicked in, and so, yeah, I needed to take a dump. This debate through the bathroom door went on for several more sentences, none of which need to be shared here, but finally she left me alone.

When the shed was "as good as it's gonna get, I guess," Mrs.

Deckle sent me home, promising to pay my parents the next day. She must've been worried that I was going to squander my hard-earned cash by betting on cockfights or something. (Yes, I recognize that not long ago I'd stolen money from my dad to buy an illegal gun, so Mrs. Deckle's concerns about my fiscal responsibility were valid.)

I rode my bicycle home, thinking that a hard day's work was supposed to bring a greater sense of personal satisfaction. Yes, I'd probably sweated off a couple of pounds, but I didn't feel like I'd built much character. If anything, I was more ageist than before.

As I turned the corner onto my street, I saw Markus, the kid who'd tormented me about the nudie magazine, standing in his front yard. He waved to me. I waved back. I realized that he was waving for me to stop, so I put on the brakes (some fancy-ass bicycles had the brakes on the handles, but my bike's brakes were activated by pedaling backward) and waited for him to hurry over.

"Did you hear?" he asked.

"Hear what?"

"So I guess you didn't hear."

"Hear *what?*"

"They arrested the guy who murdered Todd."

"When?"

"This afternoon."

"Who was it?"

"Somebody on Clerk Street."

Holy shit. I felt this weird combination of elation and horror. "Was his name Gerald Martin?"

"I don't know his name."

"What did he look like?"

"I wasn't there. I just heard that they took him away in a state trooper car."

"So they might not have arrested him. They might just have taken him in for questioning."

Markus looked annoyed, like I was messing up a great story. "I just thought you'd want to know, since you were friends with Todd."

"I did want to know. Thank you. Do you know anything else?"

"Nah."

I rode the rest of the way home. The "elation" part had vanished quickly, replaced entirely by horror. If Mr. Martin had been full of crap about his backup plan, this could be wonderful news, but if he hadn't been bluffing, or if he got out on bail, this could be very, very, very bad.

I didn't even bother to use the kickstand; I simply let my bike fall in the middle of our driveway as I hurried inside.

"How was work?" Dad asked, looking away from the television.

"Did you hear that Gerald Martin got arrested?"

Dad got up off the couch and turned down the TV volume. "I heard that he left his house with a trooper. I watched the news and they didn't mention it."

"It would be on the news if they actually arrested him, right?" Of course it would. The arrest of the man responsible for three child abductions over the summer would've made the six o'clock news for sure.

"Yeah," said Dad. He seemed to interpret my expression as "disappointment" and shut off the television altogether. "It doesn't mean they *won't* arrest him. Or maybe they did and they're keeping it quiet. He'll eventually be punished, I promise."

"I'm going to take a shower."

In the bathroom, I stripped out of my sweat-soaked, dirt-laden, and slapped-mosquito-covered clothes. What the hell should I do? This could actually be fantastic news. In fact, I could go to the authorities, tell them everything that had happened, and pile that on to whatever new information had allowed them to take Mr. Martin away. This could be the end of him.

But what if they didn't have enough evidence to arrest him? What if they didn't believe me? What if he'd gone to the station to give his statement about the psychotic fourteen-year-old who'd come over and held him at gunpoint?

He hadn't given me any definitive details, nothing that would lead to where the bodies were buried. He could say, "Yes, I told the kid these things, but he had a gun on me—what was I *supposed* to say?" Nobody else was in the room during our conversation. I was the only one who stared at his face as he spoke, who knew for certain that his confession had been real.

Would sharing the truth make things worse?

I hated to choose an official plan of action that was "do nothing for now," but it seemed like the wisest move...or, lack of a move, I guess. If Mr. Martin was placed under arrest for the abductions, I'd blab every detail of what I knew, and explain that my parents and I might be in serious danger.

If they let him go, I'd find out what happened. This might require me to talk to him again, to try to smooth things over, which was not ideal, but I'd do it if necessary.

Unfortunately, I'd have to wait until after school tomorrow. I was on thin enough ice that playing hooky my second week back would be disastrous. My mom left for the bank after I left for school, so trying to sneak out fifteen minutes early so I could ride over and check on Mr. Martin before the bus got here wouldn't work. Unless there was some sort of update in *The Daily News Miner* in the morning, I'd be in a news vacuum until tomorrow afternoon.

Maybe everything would be all right. Maybe they'd found one or more of the bodies and Mr. Martin was totally screwed.

I took a very long shower, got in my pajamas, and then

remembered that it was only seven-thirty and that I was ravenous. Mom and Dad had already eaten but she'd made me a plate of fried chicken, which I gobbled down like a fat kid who'd been building a shed all day. Then I watched TV with my parents—constantly waiting for the news to interrupt with a breaking bulletin—until it was time for bed.

My body was exhausted. My brain was on fire. My body won.

1 2

When I stepped off the bus the next morning, Tina was waiting for me.

I don't mean that she was standing right there on the sidewalk like some frightening stalker. She was standing on the front lawn of the school, near the flagpole, but she wasn't really trying to hide that she was watching to see who got off the bus. When I did, she walked right over to me.

"My dad said yes," she told me, beaming. "I mean, he wants to meet you first, if that's all right. Maybe a study date sometime this week. I know we don't have any classes together, but we wouldn't have to study the same thing. It could just be the same subject, or not even that. Whatever we wanted to study. But he said yes, which was weird, and I didn't even have to tell him very much about you. You'll like him. He's not scary or anything."

"Oh," I said.

Tina seemed a bit thrown off by this non-reaction. "I mean, you wouldn't *have* to come over for a study date. He'd just want to meet you, so maybe you could come over early. Or if we met at the library, you could talk to him in the lobby for a few minutes. Nothing too long."

I couldn't do this.

There was a psychopath who might be planning his revenge. His friend could be on a plane at this very moment. I couldn't just go to the library with Tina as if nothing was wrong. What kind of terrible person would I be if I put her in potential danger like that? I shouldn't even be talking to her right now, in case Mr. Martin was watching me.

"I'm sorry, I won't be able to do anything," I told her.

Tina nodded. She didn't look heartbroken or angry. Her reaction, which cut me even deeper, seemed to be immediate acceptance, as if this was simply the way things worked out in her life, and there was no reason to have thought otherwise.

"Okay," she said. "Thanks for asking in the first place."

She walked toward the school entrance.

She hadn't even asked why I'd changed my mind. She probably assumed that she already knew.

I was such a piece of shit.

Technically, I was the opposite. I'd be a piece of shit if I went out with Tina knowing that she could end up in a shallow grave because of it. But I sure *felt* like a piece of shit. I should have at least made something up before she left, told her that my parents were even more uptight than her father, that I wasn't allowed to be alone with a girl until I was fifteen.

Fuck.

"She turn you down, loser?" a kid called out. I didn't know his name, but he was one of Ed's buddies.

In fact, Ed was walking toward him right now. He smacked his friend in the back of the head, really hard.

"Ow, what the hell, man?"

"Leave Curtis alone," Ed said. "He's under my protection now."

"Say what?"

"You didn't hear me? You got wax in your ears? Do you want to repeat this whole conversation, including the part where I hit you?"

His friend shook his head and walked toward the school.

"Sorry about that," Ed told me. "I meant to hit him before he said anything to you."

"It's okay."

Ed gave me a thumbs-up and called for his friend to wait up. They walked into the building together. After standing there like an idiot for a few moments, I walked into the building as well, feeling confused and shitty.

IT WAS difficult to pay attention in class. I'd be desperately trying to focus on United States history, but then I'd start to think about Mr. Martin, and then I'd start sweating and try to focus back on history, then I'd start to think about Tina, and then my stomach would hurt, and then the teacher would call on me, and I'd have to admit that I had no idea what question had been asked, and the rest of the class would snicker, and the teacher would sigh, and I'd be added to the teacher's mental "will amount to very little" list. Repeat for the first four periods.

Weirdly, I was as upset about Tina as I was Mr. Martin.

There was nothing I could do about the serial killer right now, but before lunch I thought, "Who do I think I am, Spider-Man protecting my secret identity?" Though I stood by my decision not to go out with Tina, why not explain my reasoning to her? Why let her believe that I simply didn't like her? Hell, it might also be nice to have somebody I could talk to about what was happening.

I walked into the cafeteria and looked for her. Didn't see her. We were allowed to eat outside if we wanted, as long as we stayed on school grounds, so I went out to look for her. It didn't take long to find her—she was seated by herself in the back of the school, leaning against the side of the building, a paperback book in one hand and a sandwich in the other.

"Hi," I said.

"Hi."

"What are you reading?"

She held up the book. "*A Spell For Chameleon* by Piers Anthony."

"Is it any good?"

"It's great."

"Is it all right if I sit down and talk to you?"

"If you want." Tina scooted over to make room for me, even though we had the entire side of the school building to ourselves and I could have sat on either side of her just fine. She slipped in a bookmark and set her novel aside.

Mr. Martin had not given me the impression that he was a huge risk-taker, so I couldn't imagine that he would be hiding somewhere, watching the school through binoculars, in the unlikely chance that I'd come outside during lunch. Before or after school, *maybe*, though even that wouldn't be a very smart thing for a guy accused of abducting kids to do. So it was better to talk to Tina out here than risk being overheard by nosy fellow students.

"I'm sorry," I said.

"It's okay. I understand."

"No, you don't. It's not about you. Well, it is about you, but in a good way. Well, not in a *good* way, but…" She was making me babble. I didn't typically babble. "Can you keep a secret?"

"Of course."

"I mean it. This isn't a small secret, and you might feel like you need to tell somebody. But you can't tell anybody. Not your friends, not your teachers, not your dad."

"I don't have any friends, so the first one is pretty easy," said Tina. "Is this something where I could get in trouble for not telling?"

"No. You won't get in trouble."

"Then I can keep a secret. Is it that you like boys?"

"No. Okay, you know that my friend Todd got abducted, right?"

"Yes. That's how we met. I told you that I was sorry about it."

"I know, I know. I knew that you knew." More babbling. "I'm just trying to set things up. I know who did it. I saw Todd get into his car."

"Oh my God," said Tina. "Did you call the police?"

"Yes, I told them everything that happened, and they questioned the guy who did it, but they couldn't prove anything. He's still free. So I..." I hesitated. Telling the complete story would either make me sound like a complete badass or a suicidal idiot. I didn't want Tina to think I was a suicidal idiot. But the whole "it might be nice to have somebody I could talk to about what was happening" thing wouldn't work as well if I started changing my story right away, so total honesty was the way to go.

Tina just looked at me, waiting for me to continue.

"So I bought a gun from a sleazy guy in a van, and I went over to try to get him to confess. Not confess at gunpoint—I wanted to have the gun in my backpack just in case."

"Did he confess?"

"Yes. But it was at gunpoint."

"Oh."

"It basically got all messed up, and first I had the upper hand and then he had the upper hand and it pretty much ended with both of us agreeing not to say anything. Except he said that if anything happened to him, if he got arrested, his friend who I guess is a hit man would make it so me, my mom, and my dad all had to eat out of feeding tubes."

"Oh."

"I guess yesterday the state troopers took him away. I don't know if he's in jail or not. So I can't be seen with you in public, because it would put you in danger. That's why I cancelled our date. That's what I meant when I said that it was about you but in a good way."

"All right." Tina scratched her forehead. "You don't seem like you're lying to me."

"I'm not."

"Then I need you to tell me again, but with a lot more detail."

I told her everything that had happened, from the night Todd and I had our fight until the moment I heard that Mr. Martin had been taken away. She now knew that I was the kind of person who would steal money out of his dad's safe, but it was for a good cause, right? Tina asked a lot of questions as I told my story, and she apparently had no ability whatsoever to maintain a poker face. Her eyes widened at appropriate moments, she put her hand over her mouth when I was in danger, she giggled occasionally, and there was more than one gasp.

"Your summer was way more eventful than mine," she said.

"Yeah."

"Well, we should—"

The bell rang.

Tina immediately stood up. "I can't be late. Let's talk after school. Anyway, this will give me time to think of some good advice."

She picked up her book and the sandwich she never finished and hurried into the building, not waiting for me. I didn't feel as if all of my troubles had disappeared—my troubles were still lurking, big-time—but it had been a huge relief to get to tell the complete warts-and-all version of what I'd been going through. I no longer had to suffer alone.

I spent the afternoon paying more attention in class than I had in the morning.

After school, Tina walked up to my locker. "Hi."

"Hi."

"You're right, we shouldn't be seen outside of school together. I'm not worried about him coming after me, but we have a strategic advantage if he doesn't know that we're friends. I can walk by his house and he won't suspect anything."

"I don't want you to walk by his house," I said.

"I didn't say that I was going to knock on his door. But there may be a situation where you need me to keep an eye on him from a distance. The first thing we have to do is find out if he actually got arrested. If he did, then your job is to tell the police everything you know. Every single detail."

"And what if he didn't?"

"Then I think you need to talk to him."

"What?"

"I think you need to have a conversation with him and assure him that whatever happened wasn't your fault. Make sure he knows that you can still be trusted."

"Are you trying—"

"I'm not trying to get you killed," Tina promised. "You'd have the talk outside. He's not going to murder you right there in his front yard, is he?"

"I…guess not…"

"You need to get rid of the uncertainty. Make sure you and Mr. Martin are back on the same page before we take him down."

"Whoa, hold on," I said. "I never asked you to help me take him down."

"I know you didn't. So our first step is to find out what

happened. My dad's friend works for the newspaper—he works in the classified ads section, but he'd be able to talk to somebody else at the Daily News Miner and find out if Gerald Martin was arrested. So you just need to wait for me to call you. And maybe get another gun."

"I can't get another gun," I said. "I still have to replace the money for the first one."

"What you do is you call the guy who sold you the other gun and tell him you want to buy another one. Tell him you'll pay twenty percent more. Let him negotiate you up to twenty-five. Then when he opens up the door to his van, take a picture of him and tell him that if he doesn't give you the gun for free, you'll turn him in for selling an illegal gun to a kid."

"That would be a pretty crappy thing to do."

"You'd be crossing a moral line, yeah," she admitted. "I think Todd would want you to do that."

Tina seemed energized by this whole thing. There did not appear to be any notes written on her hand. I really liked her but I was also a bit scared of her.

"I'm not going to go over there with a gun," I said. "But you're right. He's not going to attack me in his front yard in broad daylight."

"Then just wait for my call and build up your courage."

I honestly didn't know which outcome I was rooting for. Mr. Martin going to prison would be nice, and I was really starting to doubt that he was telling the truth about his backup plan. If he was back home, then Tina was probably right, I should go speak with him and smooth things over, or at least confirm that he wasn't plotting blood-soaked revenge against me.

Having another conversation with Mr. Martin had very little appeal.

But it was better than a hired killer coming after me.

I unlocked the front door and went inside, still unsure which of the two possibilities I was hoping for. I set my backpack down in the foyer and walked into the living room, where a strange man sat on the couch, pointing a gun at me.

13

"Don't scream," he told me.

I didn't scream.

The man was not dressed the way I'd envisioned a professional hitman. I had an image of a black suit, impeccably pressed without a single wrinkle out of place, and sunglasses worn indoors. This guy was in corduroy pants and an untucked light blue shirt, had a thick beard, wore wire-framed glasses, and looked very tired.

"You're Curtis, right?"

"Yes, sir."

"Oh, good. Then I'm in the right place. You need better locks on your doors. I popped the one in the back in about three seconds. I mean, obviously I can get through any lock you put on there, but what you've got now wouldn't even keep out a twitching junkie."

"All right," I said.

"I'm sure you're not the one responsible for the locks around here. But you might want to pass that on to your dad."

"I will."

He stood up and yawned. "Sorry. Jetlag."

"It's okay."

"I'm guessing that we don't have much time before your parents get home, and it would be very bad if they found us like this. It would take away some options in how this plays out. You know why I'm here, right?"

I nodded. "I didn't say anything to anybody. I swear."

"Gerald believes you. The pigs came and took him into their pen to ask some questions, but nothing they asked made him think you'd ratted him out. Seemed like they were fishing without bait. So they took him back home. And while he was rolling around in the pigsty with them, he didn't call me like he was supposed to."

It *seemed* like things were going to be okay, at least for now, but the man was still pointing a gun at my face. Maybe he was trying to lull me into a false sense of security before he pulled the trigger.

"He saved my life once," said the man. "Did he tell you that?"

"No."

"I owe him big-time. He's done some shitty things, but, hell, so have I. So have we all. Doesn't cancel out the good. Anyway, I jumped on a plane and flew my ass over here the way I'd promised. Called him when I landed. Found out it had been a false alarm."

"Right," I said. "A total false alarm. I'd never break our agreement."

The man shrugged. "Maybe. I figured, as long as I was in town, I might as well show up and talk to you, man to man. I don't know about you, but I would've been a little dubious when Gerald said he had a friend like me."

"No, I believed him."

"How come you don't have any pets?"

That was a weird, random question. "My mom's allergic."

"You don't even have a hamster in your bedroom. I checked."

"I used to have goldfish but they died. That was a few years ago."

"Most kids your age have pets. You're not giving me anything to work with. You were supposed to come home and watch me kill your dog or your cat. Show you that I'm not fucking around. I'm an animal lover, but I'll suffocate a dog to get my point across, no problem."

"I told you that I didn't say anything."

"Oh, I know, I know, and I believe you. But extra incentive can't hurt. Watching your dog's eyes bug out as it desperately tries to breathe tends to send a very memorable message. I can't believe you don't have a pet."

"Right," I said. "I don't."

"I could kill a neighbor's dog, I suppose. But I don't want people going around searching for Barky or whatever."

"You and Mr. Martin don't have anything to worry about," I assured him. "He and I made an agreement, and I have every intention of sticking to it."

The man grinned. "Good. That's good to hear. So, Curtis, do you want to know what happened when I walked out of the airport?"

"What happened?"

"I took a deep breath."

"Okay."

"Fresh air. It was wonderful. I just stood outside for a while, breathing it in. I looked around and thought to myself, damn, look at that scenery. Alaska is fuckin' beautiful. And I realized that I haven't taken a vacation in a few years. Oh, I've done some hiding out, but I haven't taken a *real* vacation since even before my divorce. And I thought, why not now? Why not spend some time in the natural beauty of Alaska? Now you may be wondering why I'm sharing this. What does it mean to you? Well, young man, it means that I'm going to be around. I'm going to be close. Maybe not lurking right outside your bedroom window…or maybe I will be. It means that if you have this sudden moment where you're feeling brave, you'd goddamn well better shove it down deep, because you can *not* protect yourself from me. Got it?"

"Yes," I said. "Absolutely. Like I keep saying, we had a deal, and I'm sticking to it."

"I'm not happy to hear that."

Had I misheard him? "You're not?"

"In my job, people usually want quick, clean kills. A lot of 'make it look like an accident.' That's fine. I understand why they want that. But it's not as satisfying as making somebody truly suffer. My perfect scenario, the kind that really gets my dick rock-hard, is when I get to take somebody to a soundproof basement and just go nuts. The sound of you and your parents screaming in absolute unbearable agony would keep me going for weeks. I'd start with your mom. Totally emasculate your dad as he has to watch me do shit to her that I bet they haven't done since you came into the picture. If you try to close your eyes, I'll slice off your eyelids. By the time I'm done, you'll be begging me to kill you just because you wouldn't want to live with those images in your head. When your mom is dead—and by then you'll only recognize her as your mother because you watched it all happen—I'll start on your dad. Am I leaving out too many details? I can include as many details as you want. I've given this a lot of thought."

I couldn't answer. I could barely keep upright. If I tried to move, I was certain that my legs would give out beneath me.

The phone rang.

We both looked over at it.

"Well, shit, that spoiled the mood," he said. "I should get going anyway. Think about what I said. Think about it a lot. Don't think about anything else. The next time you see me, it won't be another warning. It will be the beginning of the most nightmarish, horrific experience you can possibly imagine."

The phone stopped ringing.

The man lowered the gun.

"Nice to meet you in person," he said. "Gerald told me a lot about you."

He walked out of the living room and into the kitchen. A moment later, I heard him open and close the back door.

My legs gave out beneath me. I collapsed onto the floor, gasping for breath.

My lungs began to burn. I really couldn't breathe.

Oh my God, was I going to die right here on my living room floor? I tried to calm myself down, to take a slow, gentle breath, but I couldn't make it work.

I had to get up. I couldn't let Mom come home and find me like this. I'd immediately be upgraded from talking to a shrink to being locked away in an asylum.

Breathe. Just breathe.

I managed to take a shallow breath. Then another. Then another.

Okay, good. I wasn't going to die here.

I crawled over to the couch and managed to climb up onto it. Not surprisingly, I was sweating like I'd run around the block with a high fever.

I closed my eyes, focused on my breathing, and tried to calm down.

A couple of minutes later, I figured I was as calm as I could possibly get, given the circumstances.

There was no way I could convince myself that this was *good,* but it definitely made things *simpler,* right? No more wondering if Mr. Martin was bluffing. Everything was very straightforward: If I went after Mr. Martin, this psychopath would come after me and my parents.

I suddenly felt like I was going to throw up.

Puking on the living room couch would not be a good idea. I staggered out of the living room, down the hallway, and into the bathroom, where I *almost* made it to the toilet before vomiting. The second batch made it into the toilet, and then I crouched there for a while, coughing and spitting.

At least the bathroom had a tile floor. Much easier to clean up.

The phone rang while I was wiping up the generous portion of barf with toilet paper. It was most likely Tina. I didn't want to answer until I'd cleaned up the bathroom—which had stench that would make your eyes water right now—so after flushing the tissue, I wiped it down with a wet rag, and then sprayed Lysol around the room. If Mom got home before the aroma faded, she'd probably think I was trying to hide the smell of marijuana, but that was better than her suspecting the truth.

I walked out of the bathroom as the phone rang again. This time I answered. "Hello?"

"Hello, Curtis." It was most definitely not Tina.

"Uh, hi, Mr. Martin." I thought the phone receiver might slip out of my hand.

"Did you have an interesting talk with my friend?"

"Yeah."

"Did he make his point very clear?"

"Uh-huh. It was already clear, though. I don't know why they came to talk to you, but it wasn't because of me."

"I believe you."

"Thank you."

"Are you scared right now, Curtis?"

"Yes."

"I want you to really think hard about how frightened you are.

Burn it into your memory. Because the agreement that you and I have isn't just for the next few days, or weeks, or months, or years. This is for the rest of our lives. And so when you start to feel comfortable, like maybe you might not be in danger any more, I want you to remember exactly how you feel in this very moment. Do you think you can do that?"

"Yes."

"I'm glad to hear that. Really glad. I'll let you go now. You probably have homework."

Mr. Martin hung up.

I hung up as well. The receiver had a thick sheen of perspiration on it, so I wiped it off with the bottom of my shirt. And to think, for a while this had been a pretty good day.

The phone rang again. Was it Tina this time, or more taunting from Mr. Martin?

"Hello?"

"Hi, Curtis. It's Tina."

"Hi."

"I tried to call earlier but you didn't answer, and then the line was busy."

"Yeah, I know. Sorry."

"Are you okay? You don't sound okay."

"I'm not very okay, no."

"What's wrong?"

"You tell me what you found out first, though I pretty much already know."

"Gerald Martin was taken in for questioning but he wasn't arrested. Apparently he's been a suspect the entire time but they don't have enough evidence to charge him."

"Yep. I knew that."

"Now tell me what's wrong."

I told her about how my last ten minutes had gone. I almost left out the part about the man threatening to rape my mom while I watched, but no, Tina needed to know just how depraved these men were, since I was going to continue to insist that we couldn't be together outside of school.

"Oh my God," she said.

"Yeah."

"But he didn't hurt you?"

"Not physically, no. Mentally, I'm pretty much insane now."

"At least you can joke about it."

"That wasn't really a joke."

"So what's your next step?" Tina asked.

"For now? Try to make myself act normal before my parents get home. After that, homework. Hopefully I can forget about Mr. Martin long enough so that I don't get F's in every class."

"But you're not going to let him win, are you?"

"Hell no. He told me to remember how scared I am right now. And I'm not gonna lie—I'm absolutely terrified. But it doesn't matter how scared I am. I'm not giving up. I don't know when it'll happen, and it may be a long time from now, but I am going to *destroy* him."

"Good," said Tina. "I'll help."

I GOT myself more or less under control before Mom got home. If she suspected that anything was wrong…well, I'd been acting weird a lot lately, so this wasn't unusual. She asked how my day at school had gone. I told her it was fine.

I decided that for the entire month of September, I would simply ignore the problem with Mr. Martin and his psycho buddy. How long could his friend's vacation possibly last? Presumably there were people around here he could murder for money, but it would be a much smaller victim pool than he'd have in the lower forty-eight. He'd eventually have to go back. He wasn't going to permanently move to Fairbanks just to be conveniently located in case I needed to die.

And so I tried to return to a normal life.

I guess I was kind of successful, if you ignore the nightmares and the paranoia and the stomachaches that I was starting to worry might be turning into an ulcer. And also the fact that I sort of had my first girlfriend, but I was scared to be seen with her outside of school, so we couldn't really do anything except have lunch together. The extent of our physical affection was some hands-holding and the occasional kiss on the cheek. Tina was all-in on the idea of defeating a serial killer, but when I suggested hiding in an empty classroom after school so we could make out, that was a very definite no.

Like most kids, I thought of the end of summer as the day school started, but technically it was September 23rd, a Sunday.

I'd made it to autumn without getting killed.

Could I make it to winter?

14

The whole "girlfriend" thing was a challenge. We were indeed boyfriend and girlfriend, not just friends, but my parents had plenty of questions. Tina and I talked on the phone every evening for at least an hour, and this was long before the magical invention of cell phones, so my options were the one in the kitchen or the one in the living room, neither of which afforded any privacy. It's not like Mom and Dad stood there staring at me while I talked to her, but even when I lowered my voice, I had to assume that my end of the conversation was a matter of public record.

Though she was comfortable talking to me, Tina's social skills were…not fantastic. The first time my dad answered the phone, she got so flustered that she couldn't remember who she wanted to speak to and ended up hanging up on him. This did not impress him. Mom and Dad would occasionally try to engage her in small talk, but would always end up shaking their heads as they handed me the phone.

When my parents asked why I didn't invite Tina over, I blamed her dad. This was a reasonable excuse at first, since Tina was thirteen and not twenty-six, so it wasn't creepy that her father wouldn't let her go over to a boy's house. But when my parents offered chaperoned dates and that still wasn't allowed—as far as they knew—it started to get a little weird. Why wouldn't we be allowed to go get hamburgers if my parents sat a couple of booths away? They even suggested that her father join them at the restaurant, which made me worried that at some point they'd ask to talk to him directly, and they'd discover that each of the fathers were being blamed for keeping these young lovers apart.

"You're not ashamed of us, are you?" Mom asked me, smiling but not completely joking.

"No, of course not. It's her dad. He's still not over the death of her mom and he's just really overprotective right now. He'll get over it soon."

"You don't have to worry. We'd be nice to her."

"Why would I think you wouldn't be nice? Why would you even say that?"

"She seems to have trouble talking. I thought that might be part of the reason."

"She's shy. She's really shy. Not everybody can be super outgoing."

"I get it," said Mom. "I'd just like to meet my son's girlfriend. There's nothing wrong with that."

I probably wasn't going to be able to fend her off for much longer. At some point, Mom would show up at school before we got on our respective busses and demand to be introduced to her. Perhaps I should even suggest that. The extremely small chance that Mr. Martin or his buddy were spying on the building after school let out was becoming overpowered by the extremely large chance that Mom would eventually say, "Enough's enough. Time for me to meet her."

Then it was October. The nights of sunlight were long gone. The sun would rise after my alarm went off, and set early in the evening. And it was cold. High of forty-five degrees Fahrenheit, and we'd lose twenty-five degrees of that by the end of the month. I followed the official Alaskan teenager dress code of "Don't dress appropriately for the weather," so I braved the cold in jeans and an unbuttoned denim jacket.

I wasn't thinking about Todd as much.

I hadn't *forgotten* about my best friend. He just didn't occupy my every waking thought. With no further appearances from the assassin and no reason to believe that Mr. Martin was peering in my windows at night, it was more and more difficult to keep up my obsession with avenging his death.

I was still visiting Dr. Wasser every week, and those fifty minutes were when I spent the most time thinking about Todd's disappearance—and, yes, as far as Dr. Wasser knew, I still believed that Todd was missing instead of dead. Each time my mom picked me up she'd ask if I still thought the sessions were helpful, and I'd say no, not really (even though they were, sort of), and she'd ask me to stick it out for another week or two. I strongly suspected that she was waiting until she could meet Tina to release me from psychological analysis.

On the days where it occurred to me that I hadn't thought about Todd much, I'd suddenly feel like an absolute piece of crap, like I'd given up on him. But I hadn't. I still had every intention of bringing Mr. Martin to justice. Yet I had a lot of other stuff going on, too. Tina was a straight-A student, and though I'd always been a pretty good student, she made me want to do better.

I continued to do odd jobs around the neighborhood whenever I could. Dad had changed the combination of his safe, foiling my effort to sneak the occasional twenty-dollar bill in there, but the money I earned went into two piles. Half was for repaying the money I stole. (I hadn't decided yet if I would confess, or if I'd just leave a stack of bills on his desk and pretend that I had no idea how it got there; sort of a Stolen Cash Reimbursement Santa Claus.) The other half was for dates with Tina, when we could actually start dating like a real couple.

I was getting a lot of exercise, and thus losing…a *little* weight, I guess? Not much. Chubbiness seemed to be my body's natural state. Although I tended to be ravenously hungry when I got home, and I didn't reach for a head of lettuce, so that might have had something to do with it.

"What are you doing for Halloween?" Tina asked, as we spoke on the phone one evening.

"I don't know." Until the sixth grade, trick-or-treating was the entire purpose of this holiday. Costumes tended to just be the kind that came in a box, with the cheap plastic mask that covered your face but not the rest of your head. If you were Spider-Man, the suit was not Spider-Man's costume—it just had a picture of Spider-Man on the chest. I didn't care. It was usually, oh, maybe fifteen degrees outside, so a Halloween costume had to keep you warm for a couple of hours of candy gathering. It was often worn over a snowsuit. Nobody was doing elaborate makeup, because your face would freeze off if it wasn't covered.

I'd retired from trick-or-treating upon entering junior high, even though I didn't really want to. I didn't worry *too* much about society's expectations, but I sure as hell wasn't going to be the only Fairbanks teenager doing it. (I've also just admitted that upon becoming a teenager I stopped trying to protect myself from the cold weather, so, yes, I guess I was fully susceptible to being a dumbass to fit in with my peers.)

"What about a Halloween party?" Tina asked.

"Who's having one?" Despite wearing only a jeans jacket in

freezing weather, I wasn't cool enough to get invited to Halloween parties.

"You."

"Me?"

"What if you had a costume party, but only invited me and my dad? If anybody was spying on us, they wouldn't know who I was. I could finally see your house and we'd get our parents off our backs." She'd been whispering, but now she raised her voice. "My dad is starting to think that I'm making you up. Like I'm just talking to myself on the phone. At this very moment, making up an entire imaginary conversation just for his benefit."

"Did your dad just walk in the room?" I asked.

"Oh, yeah. He's staring right at me."

"I think it's a great idea. Maybe we shouldn't call it a Halloween party, it's kind of sad if we're having a party that's just us and our parents. We'll call it a Halloween gathering."

"Let's do it."

Over dinner, I shared this with my parents, both of whom loved the idea. That night, while I was brushing my teeth, my mom stood in the bathroom doorway and told me that if I wanted to stop seeing Dr. Wasser, that was fine.

Halloween was still more than three weeks away. Plenty of time to plan a very small party. Some snacks, some decorations, and whatever horror movie was playing on TV that night, if any. (Our channels consisted of CBS on Channel 11 and PBS on Channel 9, while Channel 2 was shared by both NBC and ABC. So horror movies on Halloween night weren't a guarantee.)

Quite honestly, the whole "Tina cannot be seen with me for fear that she might become a pawn in my standoff against Mr. Martin" was starting to feel kind of silly. Could she *really* only come over if she was in a Halloween costume? It was getting extremely cold out. Where would Mr. Martin and his friend even be hiding to watch us? Wouldn't he be worried that I'd go straight to the authorities if I caught him spying?

Maybe all of these precautions were ridiculous.

But maybe they weren't. I didn't know how Mr. Martin's mind worked. Though I assumed that he was still going to his job, an insane child killer like him might indeed be watching me as often as he could. Maybe his friend was driving by my house every once in a while.

I had to stay vigilant, even if it might be a waste of time.

This wouldn't last forever. Eventually I'd get him.

OCTOBER ALWAYS BROUGHT a few days of snowfall that melted away, but by Halloween the snow was there to stay for the rest of the winter and beyond. Each day we lost six or seven minutes of daylight, down to less than eight hours by Halloween. At least we still had a couple of daylight hours after school let out—in the coming months, it would be pitch black when the bus arrived, and pitch black when the bus left.

My parents and I decided to make our own costumes. Since we weren't going anywhere, they didn't have to be cold-resistant. I dressed as a hobo, because this was back when you would say "hobo" instead of "homeless person." (And you didn't really see homeless people in Alaska in the winter.) My mom was a green-faced witch. My dad was Chewbacca, though he looked more like Bigfoot with mange.

We had popcorn, chips, cookies, and candy galore. Our neighborhood always had a lot of trick-or-treaters, and we gave out the good stuff, Snickers and M&M's. No apples or that orange-and-black-wrapped peanut butter taffy.

Tina and her dad arrived, and they'd put a lot more effort into their costumes. Tina was a devil, with sparkles all over her outfit, three different shades of red makeup (blended exquisitely) and a tail that she could move around with a pulley system attached to her back. Her dad was also a hobo, but a much more elaborate one. He'd blacked out some of his teeth and had a long stick with his possessions tied up in a handkerchief on the end. "I was going to go for authentic body odor, but Tina talked me out of it," he said, laughing.

Tina's dad was shockingly cool. I'm not saying that I wanted him to adopt me, since that would technically make Tina and I brother and sister, but he was far different from what I'd expected, which was either a drill sergeant or somebody who looked like a raincloud should be following him everywhere. Here, he was the life of the party, offering up a constant stream of jokes, eating an alarming amount of junk food, and praising the costume artistry of every single trick-or-treater who came to the door.

After a slow start, Tina also started to have fun. She shared a couple of amusing anecdotes about past Halloween experiences, and yes, I could tell she'd practiced them, perhaps for hours. My parents adored her.

It's entirely possible that most people in my peer group would think that a Halloween party that consisted of two kids and three parents was lame as hell, but screw it. Everybody was having a great time.

"I'm so glad we finally got to meet you," said Mom. "It feels like we've been waiting for this forever."

"Yeah, yeah," said Tina's dad. "Tina has told me so much about Curtis, and I've been anxious to find out if he lived up to the hype. He completely does. Exceeds expectations."

Tina and I exchanged a concerned look, because this was the part where our parents might start to compare stories, which could be problematic. But then the doorbell rang, and they went over to hand some candy to a ghost and a pirate, and when they returned the subject didn't come back up. We'd dodged a bullet. This was the best Halloween party ever.

This was not an alcohol-free party for the adults. Around nine o'clock, Tina's dad declined another beer, since he had to drive home, but my dad sent me to the kitchen to get another one for him and Mom. They had to go to work tomorrow (it was Wednesday; Halloween was celebrated on October 31st regardless of which day of the week it fell upon—no pushing it to the weekend in Fairbanks in 1979) but it's not like they were getting sloppy drunk. Tina went with me.

"This is so great," she said. "I can't believe how much fun Dad is having. He's usually so gloomy."

"Maybe we can relax a little. I don't mean holding hands in front of Mr. Martin's house, but are we being too paranoid? I haven't heard anything from him in almost a month."

Tina shrugged. "Maybe. You know him better than I do."

We stared at each other for a very long moment.

"Do you want to make out?" I asked.

"It'll smear my devil makeup."

"That's true. Sorry. I wasn't thinking."

"You can touch one of my boobs if you do it quick."

"Hey!" my dad called out. "I'm sitting here without a beer!" The other adults laughed. My parents didn't get tipsy very often, so I was glad that they were enjoying themselves, even if my dad's timing sucked crap.

I got the beer out of the refrigerator and Tina and I returned to the party. The low lighting and my baggy outfit was a godsend, because at that age I could get a boner from a female teacher writing the number 8 on the blackboard, so Tina's offer had put me in a physical condition that her father would not appreciate.

At nine-thirty, there was a knock at the door. We hadn't turned off the porch light, but trick-or-treaters didn't generally show up after nine. My mom got up and answered.

It wasn't a kid in a costume. It was a frantic-looking woman in a parka.

I thought I recognized her. I couldn't tell you where I'd seen her before, but I was pretty sure she lived in my neighborhood.

"Sorry to bother you so late," she said. "Did you have a trick-or-treater in a skeleton costume tonight?"

"I…think so," Mom told her. "We had a lot of kids tonight. There was at least one skeleton."

"I sewed the fabric bones onto his dark blue jacket, and he would've been wearing red glasses that lit up."

"I would've remembered the red light-up glasses," said Mom. She looked back at the rest of us. "Do any of you remember a skeleton trick-or-treater?"

None of us did.

"Okay," the woman said. "Just thought I'd check."

"What happened?" Mom asked.

"My son never came home."

"Oh my God. How old is he?"

"Eleven. He got separated from his friends, I guess. They don't know what happened to him."

"Well, give me your phone number and I'll call you if we see him."

"Thank you." The woman wiped a tear from her eye. I was surprised it didn't freeze to her face.

Her son was named Dominick. I didn't know him very well—he was three years younger than me—but I knew that he lived about five blocks away. I wondered if his mother had gone to every house between theirs and ours. She said she'd called 911, and her husband was waiting at home for word.

And on that bummer of a note, Tina's dad announced that they needed to go since she had school tomorrow. Goodbyes were exchanged, and everybody agreed that we needed to do this again, minus the Halloween costumes.

My plan to just kind of forget about Mr. Martin for a while had failed. Now I had to figure out what to do about him.

15

Not being a sixteen-year-old with a driver's license in the twenty-first century made this situation much more challenging. I couldn't just secretly text or e-mail Tina. We couldn't even lower the volume on the phone's ringer—those things were designed to make sure you *knew* that somebody was calling.

My parents went to bed shortly after Tina and her dad left. I waited until they'd have made it home, then called from the kitchen phone. If Mom or Dad came out of their bedroom to ask why I was calling her, I'd say that she'd promised to bring *A Spell for Chameleon* to school tomorrow for me to borrow, and I didn't want her to forget.

"Hello?" her dad answered.

"Hi," I said. "It's Curtis. May I speak to Tina?"

"What, you don't want to talk to me?" He chuckled. "Yeah, but make it quick. You both have school in the morning."

"Hi," said Tina, a moment later. Her grim tone made it clear that she knew why I was calling.

I lowered my voice to a whisper. "I'm going over there."

"Right now?"

"Yes. If I wait until morning, it might be too late."

"Can't you just call the police?"

"Dominick's mom said she already did. I assume he'd be their prime suspect, so they might already be investigating him. If I get over there and I see state troopers parked in his driveway, I'll come home. But I can't just go to sleep until I've tried to do something to help."

"I don't know how to get over there," said Tina. "My dad is watching TV. There's no way I can sneak out. And if I wait until he goes to sleep, I'll have to go to a pay phone to call a cab. I could tell him what's going on, but—"

"I'm not asking you to come over here. There's no time for that." I did some mental calculations. I could get to Mr. Martin's house in about ten minutes if I ran the entire way. I probably couldn't run the entire way, so maybe fifteen minutes. If things went badly, I wanted the state troopers on their way to save me as soon as possible, but I didn't want Tina to call them before it was necessary. How long should I ask her to wait? "Give me one hour. If I haven't called by then, call 911 and tell them where I am."

"Are you sure you want to do this?" asked Tina. "Going over to a serial killer's house after dark? Is this really your responsibility?"

"It's my fault Todd was killed," I said. "I'm not going to let something like that happen again."

I was kind of surprised at myself for saying that. I regretted the fight we'd had that sent Todd walking home on his own, but I'd never really been wallowing in self-blame. Was this some kind of buried guilt? Why hadn't Dr. Wasser dragged it out of me?

Didn't matter. Yes, I was going to confront Mr. Martin...as safely as possible.

"I understand," said Tina. "Are you bringing a gun?"

"No."

"A knife?"

"I guess I should bring a knife."

"Be careful, Curtis."

"Oh, I will. I'll be completely safe, I promise. I'll talk to you in less than an hour."

I hung up. I slid open one of the kitchen drawers and selected a knife, the one my mom used for cutting vegetables. My dad had a pocketknife in his desk in his office, but I wanted to sneak around the house as little as possible. I put on a pair of boots (which I'd never wear to school where my peers could see me, of course, but I was going to have to move quickly and I didn't want to slip on the ice) and then opened the closet door. I selected a heavy jacket, put it on, and slipped the knife into the pocket.

Did I *really* want to do this?

No. Not at all. But I was going to anyway.

I returned to the kitchen and very slowly turned the doorknob. Then I very, very slowly eased the door open. The stupid thing creaked of course, which in my state of anxiety felt like it was shaking the entire house and waking up everybody on our block. I continued to swing the door open until I could slip through, and then I just as carefully closed it.

I trudged through the snow in our yard, walking around the side of the house. I suddenly realized just how *dark* it was out here.

My stomach hurt. I didn't want to do this. Tina was right—why was this my responsibility? Why was I, a fourteen-year-old kid, on my way to try to rescue somebody from a serial killer? What kind of bullshit was that?

I was on my way over there because I was the one who'd forced Mr. Martin to confess at gunpoint and then proceeded to squander my advantage. I was on my way over there because I'd screwed up. Simple as that.

I started to run, then decided that this would end with me slipping and breaking a leg or two. I settled for jogging. Despite the exercise I'd been getting from doing odd jobs, I was still in terrible shape—all of the junk food I'd eaten this evening didn't help—and it wasn't long before I got a cramp in my side. I fought through it and kept jogging.

To be clear, my intentions were not to kick down Mr. Martin's door, rush inside, and save the kidnapped child. Self-preservation was an important part of my plan. I was on my way to gather information that I could use to send the authorities after him, not to perform a daring rescue. This wasn't an "exchange my life for Dominick's" expedition.

By the time I'd reached the end of my neighborhood, I had to stop jogging and settle for a relatively quick walk. I couldn't show up at Mr. Martin's home gasping for breath.

I suddenly wondered if I should've left my parents a quick note, in case they got up and discovered that I was gone. Too late now.

This was such a stupid idea. Only a mentally ill person would be doing something like this. How could Tina even want to be my girlfriend? How could I have been seeing a shrink for all those weeks and still have a brain that would let me do something this dumb?

I didn't turn back.

When I turned onto Mr. Martin's street, I slowed way down—not out of cowardice, but to make sure I could speak calmly and articulately when he answered his door. I reached his house and decided against this whole ridiculous idea. But before I could turn around and start walking back home, I forced myself to walk up to his front door and ring the doorbell.

I quickly hurried back, about twenty feet away.

Nobody answered.

I repeated the process.

Still no answer.

If he wasn't home, I had to assume that he had Dominick with him.

I walked up to the front door and began to pound on it.

A light turned on inside.

I retreated back to what I hoped was a safe distance.

The door opened. Mr. Martin was in a robe. His hair stuck up on the left side. As he saw me, he rubbed his eyes and let out a soft groan.

"Is that you, Curtis?"

"Yeah."

"What the hell do you want?" he asked.

"Turn on your porch light."

"Why?"

"So that we aren't talking in the dark."

He turned on the light. I could see that a couple of the other homes had lights on inside, so hopefully that would dissuade him from coming after me. He *might* be able to knock me unconscious and drag me into his home without anybody noticing, but I doubted he'd take the risk.

I also noticed some yellow streaks and white fragments on his windows. He'd been egged. He must not have handed out treats this evening.

"I have to get up early tomorrow," he said, stepping outside.

"Stay in your house or I'll start screaming," I warned him.

Mr. Martin took a step back. "Tell me what this is about or I'll call the cops. Have you arrested for disorderly conduct."

"Another kid is missing."

"Who?"

"You tell me."

149

"No, *you* tell *me*. I don't know anything about a missing kid. I haven't left the house tonight."

Honestly, he sounded like he was telling the truth.

"So you're saying it's a coincidence that another kid disappeared?"

Mr. Martin glanced around, as if making sure nobody else could hear him. "Yes, that is exactly what I'm saying."

"I don't believe you."

"Did you call the cops?"

"No."

"You sure?"

"I'm sure. But the kid's mother did."

"More harassment on the way for me, huh? Wonderful. I love operating heavy machinery without any sleep. What did you hope to gain here? Did you think I was just going to burst into tears and confess?"

"I thought I'd be able to tell if you were lying."

"Well, your internal bullshit detector is all messed up. It's Halloween night. A lot of stuff could happen to a kid."

"All right," I said. "I guess we're done, then."

Mr. Martin didn't look like a sadistic killer hiding a secret. He looked like a guy who was genuinely annoyed at being woken up when he had to get up early for work the next morning.

"Are we?" he asked.

"Yeah."

He stepped outside again.

"Stay in your house," I told him.

He took a step closer.

"Stay back or I'll make a lot of noise," I warned.

"Then scream. People will think it's some obnoxious little brat trying to get in a last scare on Halloween. I'm not going to hurt you, but I've got some more things to say."

He continued walking toward me. I spun around to try to flee, and my foot came right down on a patch of ice. I flailed my arms wildly to try to keep my balance but there was nothing to grab onto, and I fell on my ass.

As I tried to scoot away, Mr. Martin crouched down. He wasn't close enough for me to stab him. I decided not to scream quite yet.

"We have a problem here," he informed me. "I don't like that you think you can just come over here, pound on my door, and accuse me of something I didn't do. This makes me think that you feel like you're the one in charge here. That doesn't work for me."

"If a kid goes missing, yeah, I'm going to assume you did it," I said.

"I get that. I really do. But this little power struggle we've got going on here is not balanced in your favor. You understand that, right? You can make life difficult for me, but I can make life so much worse, and so much shorter for you."

I scooted back further.

"Don't move," he said. "We're not done talking. You started this up again, so you're goddamn well going to listen to what I have to say. *You* are the one living in fear. Not me. I sleep fine, unless some rotten little shit starts pounding on my door. Do you think I flinch when the phone rings? Is that what you think? Do you think I'm always peeking out the windows?"

I shook my head.

"I'm not your little bitch. If you break our agreement, it will be *so* much worse for you than for me. I assumed that you understood that, but I guess I was wrong."

"I understand," I said.

"Do you?"

"Yes."

"Maybe it's too late." He glanced around. "You think anybody hears us? You think anybody is watching right now? Maybe you fucked this up beyond repair. Maybe I have nothing to lose."

"Nobody's watching."

"You sure about that? If you're right, then why shouldn't I shove your face in the snow until you suffocate, then drag your fat ass into my house? Let your body feed me during the long winter. How does that sound? Maybe we should just fight it out, right here, right now. Give the neighbors a Halloween to remember? Did you bring a gun this time? Why don't you shoot me? C'mon, Curtis, if you're such a big man, go ahead and shoot me? Shoot me in the face. See if my blood freezes before it hits the ground. Do it. Shoot me. Do it."

"I made a mistake," I said. I slid my hand into my jacket pocket, wincing as my fingers slid across the blade.

Mr. Martin grinned. "You really are going for a gun, huh?"

"No."

"Okay. I trust you. I thought things were fine between us, Curtis. I thought we were on the same page. It's hard for me to explain how upsetting this is. But you know what? Go ahead and end the game. Turn me in. Tell whoever the fuck you want about me. See how well it works out. You want to use my phone? Come on in. I'll get you some milk and cookies while you call. How does that sound?"

"I'm sorry," I said. "I messed up."

"Oh, well, if you're sorry, I guess everything is just hunky dory, huh?"

"A kid disappeared tonight. I freaked out."

"Well, how about in the future you *don't* freak out, okay?"

I slowly got to my feet. "It won't happen again."

"Good to know."

"I'm leaving now."

"Sleep well. Happy Halloween."

Mr. Martin walked back into his house, shutting the door behind him. The porch light turned off, followed by the light inside his house.

I'd made things even worse, but I was also weirdly relieved that —as far as I could tell—he hadn't been responsible for Dominick's disappearance. Maybe Dominick was home by now, fast asleep in his bed.

Now to get home and call Tina.

I hadn't even walked past his next-door neighbor's house before I slipped on another patch of ice. My leg twisted as I fell. I cried out in pain as I hit the ground.

I wiggled my toes. My leg wasn't broken, but God, did it hurt.

After a few tries, I managed to get back up. Then I limped toward home.

I still had forty minutes. Thirty-nine, if Tina called exactly at the one-hour mark. I'd make it, no problem.

At the end of the block, my injured leg shot out from under me and I fell again.

Got back up.

Every step hurt, but I forced myself to keep going. Worst case scenario, I'd pound on somebody's door and ask to borrow their phone.

I made it home with about seven minutes to spare. The lights weren't on inside the house. I walked around to the back door, and once again very, very slowly opened it. Then closed it, wondering if this was seriously the loudest fucking door on the planet.

"Curtis…?" my mom called out.

"Sorry!" I answered. "Just getting a drink."

She didn't answer. I quickly but quietly got out of my jacket, then bent down and untied my boots, listening carefully for footsteps. I had no cover story if she walked into the kitchen and saw me changing.

153

The living room light turned on.

Shit!

I continued to untie the boots, praying that Mom wouldn't walk into the kitchen to check on me or get a drink of her own.

The television turned on.

I slipped off the boots, which now felt like they were attached to my feet with the suction of a thousand vacuum cleaners, and set them out of the way. There was nowhere in the kitchen to hide my jacket or boots.

I was acutely aware of how many steps were involved in the task of getting a glass of water. Open the cabinet. Take down a glass. Turn on the faucet. Hold the glass under the stream of water. All while waiting for my mom to walk into the kitchen and ask why my jacket and boots were on the floor.

I shut off the faucet and walked into the living room.

"I can't sleep," said Mom, looking over at me. "Too much excitement, I guess. And I'm worried about Dominick." She frowned. "Are you okay?"

"Yeah, why?"

"Your face is bright red."

"My makeup wouldn't come off. I had to scrub really hard."

My hobo makeup was just supposed to look like I had a dirty face and had come off easily with soap and water. The timing was suspect—why would I have waited until now to take it off?—and I'm sure my ears were bright red from the cold, too. This story could completely fall apart with a single follow-up question.

"Okay," said Mom. "You should go to bed."

"I will."

I couldn't sneak back into the kitchen and quietly make a phone call. It had a rotary dial. Those things were noisy. Shit.

"I need to call Tina," I said.

"This late?"

"Yeah. I let her borrow one of my books, but I need it for an open-book quiz tomorrow, so I need to make sure she remembers to bring it."

"She wouldn't forget something like that, would she? She's not going to leave your school book at home."

"She might."

"It's eleven o'clock. Call her in the morning before she gets on the bus."

"It's fine. She stays up late. It'll be quick." I stepped back into the kitchen, taking the calculated risk that my mom wouldn't rush in there and knock the phone out of my hand.

I dialed Tina's number. She answered instantly after the first ring.

"Hey, Tina, it's me," I said. "I just wanted to make sure you didn't forget my math book tomorrow."

"Did it go okay?" Tina whispered.

"Yep, I had a great time, too. Tell your dad I said hi. See you tomorrow."

I hung up. If Mom had been trying to overhear my conversation, and I assumed that she was, that shouldn't have sounded too suspicious. But I had no idea what to do with the jacket and boots. I couldn't put them outside, because there was no conceivable reason that I'd need to open the back door. If I told Mom that I thought I saw something outside, she'd come to check it out as well.

I'd simply have to leave them there and hope that Mom didn't come into the kitchen. Then I'd set my alarm for a couple of hours from now, and put them back in the closet after she went to sleep.

I stepped into the living room. "She said she won't forget. I'm going to bed now."

Mom looked over at me. "Good night."

I hesitated for just a moment, hoping she'd return her attention to the television. She didn't. She kept looking at me. I couldn't keep standing there like an idiot, so I'd have to walk across the living room toward the stairs. This was problematic, since my leg was still killing me and I wasn't sure I could do it without limping.

I tried to harness my inner ballerina and walk with grace.

"You okay?" Mom asked.

"Why?"

"You're walking funny."

"I banged my leg on the counter. I was trying not to wake you up, so I didn't turn the light on in the kitchen."

"Do you want me to take a look?"

"Nah, it's fine."

Mom got up off the couch. "I'll get you an ice pack."

"It's totally fine. I won't be able to sleep if I have an ice pack on it. It doesn't hurt at all."

"You sure?"

"Yep. I love you. Good night." I resumed walking, praying that she wouldn't decide that I was incapable of making my own decisions about leg care and get an ice pack anyway.

I walked upstairs, grimacing with each step. I went into my bedroom, shut the door, and took off my pants. My leg was swelling up pretty badly. Great. Maybe I would ice it down, after Mom went to bed.

I got undressed the rest of the way, shut off the light, and climbed into bed.

I kept screwing things up. But I had to go over there, right? What if Mr. Martin *had* kidnapped Dominick, and I didn't find out until tomorrow morning? How could I have lived with myself knowing that I could've done something to save him?

I couldn't sleep, of course, so I lay in bed until I heard Mom shut off the television. I waited exactly fifteen minutes after that, then snuck back downstairs and put the boots and jacket back into the closet. I put the knife back in the drawer. I got an ice pack out of the freezer and took it back to my bedroom. I left it on my leg until it was no longer cold, and it seemed to help quite a bit. Finally, I fell asleep.

The next morning, Dominick was found dead.

16

It wasn't clear how Dominick met his fate, but kids all over school were talking about the boy who'd frozen to death on Halloween night. There was no evidence of foul play. He'd been found in a neighbor's backyard, along the route Dominick might have followed if he'd been taking a shortcut to get back to his own house.

His footprints were the only set—nobody had been with him. The footprints stopped a few yards away from his body, replaced by a thick track, as if he'd begun to crawl.

One of the friends who'd been trick-or-treating with him mentioned that Dominick had complained that he wasn't feeling well. Apparently he'd been much sicker than simply having a bellyache from too much candy.

There was absolutely no evidence that it had anything to do with Mr. Martin. It was a tragedy that would haunt our area for a long time, but it wasn't the work of a serial killer.

As we stood by her locker, I told Tina everything that had happened.

"I get why you went over there," she said. "But you have to promise me you won't do it again. Not by yourself."

"I'm not taking you with me."

"Okay, but I can wait nearby. A lot could've happened in an hour. You could've been long-dead before anybody showed up to save you."

"You're right," I said. "I just didn't have a choice."

"Do you think he'll try anything?"

I shrugged. "He was acting crazy last night, but hopefully he's calmed down. He knows that I'm not going to let him get away with anything. He tried to pretend that he doesn't care if I go to the police, but that can't possibly be true. I think he'll be on his best behavior."

"For how long?"

"I don't know. Maybe he'll move away. Why would he even want to live here anymore? If I had somebody like me pounding on my door late at night accusing me of that kind of stuff, I'd move someplace else."

"That would be great if he just left," said Tina. "Maybe we can figure out a way to make that happen."

"Of course, we'd be sending him to a new place with a whole new pool of victims. It might be better for him to stick around here so I can keep an eye on him."

Tina sighed. "Yeah, you're right. My dad really liked you, by the way."

"Really? He didn't say, 'My God, what a complete loser! How could you possibly be attracted to somebody who's never going to amount to anything? He's gross! He's totally gross!'?"

"Nope, he sure didn't."

"Cool."

"He knows that I have flawless taste."

I smiled, but the smile quickly faded. "I think last night reset the whole thing with Mr. Martin. We have to assume that he's paying close attention to me again. So I guess we're back to saying that we shouldn't be seen together outside of school."

"I didn't realize we'd changed that, outside of Halloween costumes."

"We hadn't. But I was going to bring up the idea."

The first bell rang and we hurried off to class. This would've been an agonizingly long day even under good circumstances, simply because it was hard to get back into the vibe of education the day after Halloween. The death of Dominick, even though I didn't know him very well, and my latest encounter with Mr. Martin were going to weigh on my mind for the foreseeable future.

I couldn't let this go on forever.

When you're a kid, you don't think in terms of "my childhood is being stolen." But I was getting tired of Mr. Martin ruining my life. It was November 1st. We were almost at the end of the decade (pedantic cries of "the end of the decade is technically December 31st, 1980" notwithstanding) and I wasn't going to start the 1980's living in fear of that asshole. I was going to finish this. Somehow.

The mood was grim at home. We didn't know Dominick very well, but still, when an eleven-year-old dies in your area, in a city not really known for its shocking tragedies, it carries a lot of weight.

I was too exhausted to have another sleepless night. I still woke up a couple of times, unable to shake the weird feeling that somebody was in the house, but when I crept around to investigate, I saw nothing unusual. Maybe it was Dominick's ghost.

The next day was Friday, which was normally cause for celebration except that I had *three* different tests, none of which had received the level of studying that they required. (If I'd been a teacher, I would've shown my students mercy and not scheduled tests on Halloween week, but I was not consulted on the matter.)

Second period was Pre-Algebra. I stared at the test. The

formulas on the page looked as foreign as…well, algebra. This was going to be ugly.

Somebody knocked on the classroom door.

Mrs. Van Lauren glanced over from her desk and scowled. She believed that algebra was the engine that drove all of humanity, so if somebody was interrupting her test, it had better be extremely important. She pushed back her chair, but the door opened before she finished getting up.

Principal Taylor walked into the classroom. He seemed to suddenly realize that he was interrupting a test, so he quietly walked over to Mrs. Van Lauren and whispered something to her. Both of them looked over at me.

It became very difficult to breathe.

I'm not sure why my mind immediately went to *Oh, shit, I'm in trouble.* Maybe Mr. Martin had finally been arrested and they needed my statement. This could be good.

Principal Taylor didn't look like this was good.

He walked over to my desk. "Curtis, I'll need you to come with me."

I nodded. "Okay."

"Bring your things."

I picked up my backpack and stood up. We walked toward the door.

"Eyes on your work," Mrs. Van Lauren announced, but of course every eye was on me.

Maybe I wasn't in trouble. Maybe something horrible had happened.

Maybe Tina was dead. Maybe Mom and Dad were dead.

I should never have gone over there.

We walked out into the hallway. "What's wrong?" I asked. Principal Taylor didn't answer. He was walking so quickly that I had to jog a little to keep up.

When we went around the corner, I saw a state trooper standing by my locker.

If they just wanted to question me, or deliver bad news, why would he be standing by my locker?

At least nobody was dead.

We walked over there. "Here he is," said Principal Taylor, as if the trooper might not have noticed that he had a student with him.

The trooper gave me a stern nod. "Hello, Curtis. I'm going to need you to open your locker."

There was absolutely nothing in my locker that I'd want to hide from the principal or the authorities. At least, there hadn't been before. I suddenly had a very good idea of where this might be headed.

My mind went blank and I couldn't remember my locker combination. I closed my eyes and spent a moment trying to focus.

"Do it," said Principal Taylor, mistaking my erased memory for reluctance.

I turned the dial, hoping the combination would come back to me when my fingers started moving. It did. I unlocked it, then pulled open the door. As it swung open, I half-expected to see a severed head dangling in there, but the inside of my locker looked the same as it had this morning. Messy as hell.

"Please move away," the trooper told me.

I stepped out of the way. The trooper began to methodically search through my locker.

"What are you looking for?" I asked. Principal Taylor shushed me.

It took at least ten excruciating minutes for the trooper to finish going through my stuff. Finally he reached for my backpack. "Hand it over, please."

I gave him my backpack.

Everything was going to be fine. I'd had my backpack with me all day. Nobody would have had a chance to slip anything in there without me noticing.

Unless I *hadn't* imagined that somebody was in the house last night.

Oh, God.

Mr. Martin wouldn't do anything like this, would he? What would he gain? Why would he do something that would force me to tell the authorities what I knew? This all had to be a huge misunderstanding. The state trooper would go through my backpack, apologize, and then I'd return to class so Mrs. Van Lauren and I could figure out what we were going to do about the pre-algebra test that I'd abandoned.

The trooper unzipped my backpack and began taking things out and setting them on the floor. Books. Pencils. A notebook. An empty can of root beer that I'd meant to throw away a couple of weeks ago. Some empty potato chip bags. When I got out of this mess, I'd have to start cleaning out my backpack on a regular basis.

"Oops," said the trooper. "Yep, here we go."

He took out a large baggie filled with what I immediately knew —without ever having seen any in real life—was marijuana.

"That's not mine," I insisted.

"Of course it's not."

"Somebody put that in there."

"Of course they did." The trooper, instead of looking gleeful at his discovery, seemed genuinely disappointed in me. "Do I need to use handcuffs, or are you going to come with me without any fuss?"

I informed him that I wouldn't cause any problems.

THE BELL RANG before we made it out of the building, which meant that plenty of my peers got to see me led out of the school and into the waiting car.

No good could come from telling my story to the trooper while we were in transit. He wasn't going to say, "Wait, you're telling me that Gerald Martin planted this on you? Oh my goodness! Well, let me send you right back to class so I can capture the real criminal!"

I was taken into the station, fingerprinted, and placed in a holding cell. At least I got a cell of my own, though there was plenty of snickering from the adjacent cell, probably because of my constant sniffling as I desperately tried not to cry.

Mom and Dad showed up a while later. I thought they were there to take me home to be grounded for the rest of my life, but instead they just stood outside the cell.

"Why would you do this?" Mom asked. "How would it ever even occur to you to sell drugs?"

"The bag wasn't mine," I insisted. "Somebody stuck it in there."

"Who?"

I hesitated. This was going to sound crazy. "Gerald Martin."

"You're saying that Gerald Martin put a bag of weed in your backpack?"

"Yes."

"And then he called the police, pretending to be a concerned parent of a student who was one of your customers?"

"Yes!"

"How would he get it in there?"

"I don't know! He has a friend. I think his friend broke into…" I realized that this theory was not being well received and just trailed off. "I confronted Mr. Martin about Todd's disappearance, and now he's trying to get back at me."

"You did *what?*" Dad asked.

"I went over there. He admitted what he did. And then I went over again on Halloween night because I thought he was responsible for Dominick going missing. I'm not selling pot. He or his friend put that in my backpack. Where would I even get that much pot? How could I afford it?"

"You stole money out of my safe," said Dad.

My stomach plummeted.

"Or did Gerald Martin's friend break into our house and steal that, too?"

My mind raced. Should I accept that I was screwed and stop talking? *Yes, Father, I stole the money, but only so I could buy an illegal gun with which to force a confession out of Mr. Martin.* Was that more credible than the idea that I stole money to buy marijuana to sell to kids at school?

For now, I needed to just shut the hell up.

"We're going to have to hire a lawyer," Mom told me. "Your father and I think it will do you good to spend the night here."

"What? You're going to leave me in jail?"

"Just for one night."

"No!"

"Talking to a psychiatrist didn't work," said Mom, a tear trickling down her cheek. "What we're doing clearly isn't working. We know how devastated you are by what happened to your friend, but that's no excuse. If we found a stash of cigarettes in your room, that would be different. They found a *lot* of marijuana in your backpack. That's intention to sell."

"It wasn't mine."

"We'll come back for you in the morning."

I wanted to start screaming and begging for her not to leave me, but something else was more important. "Be careful," I said. "It's not enough to lock the doors. Sleep in shifts. Have a gun by the bed. He might come for you."

"Curtis—"

"Promise me you'll be careful. Maybe stay at a hotel or something. If you're going to leave me to rot in jail, you at least have to swear that you'll protect yourselves tonight."

"We're not leaving you to rot," said Dad.

"Just promise me."

"We'll be safe. Worry about yourself for now."

"No!" I shouted. "I'm fucking worried about *you!*"

This was the first time I'd cursed in front of my parents. I'd known the day was coming, but hadn't expected it to be while I was behind bars.

They left.

I plopped down on the bench.

"Whoooo-eeeeee, that's rough," said a guy in the next cell. He had greasy hair, a terrible complexion, and bad teeth. "We'll take care of you, don't worry."

I began to cry.

When it turned into an all-out sobbing fit, the guy apparently took pity on me and walked to the other side of his cell to give me some privacy.

A couple of hours later, they moved me from the holding cell to a cell with a toilet and something close to a bed.

I prayed that my parents would take my warning seriously.

They served lunch and dinner. I assumed that both of them tasted disgusting from the look and smell, but I couldn't have eaten even if I'd been presented with Thanksgiving dinner with all the trimmings.

After they shut out the lights, I lay on the bed, frightened about pretty much everything.

17

Mom took pity on me, picking me up at six in the morning. I'd been crying much of the night, stopping only when the greasy guy told me to shut the fuck up, and the tears started again when I saw her.

I didn't have a court date yet. I had a meeting with a lawyer set for Wednesday afternoon.

The stolen money was a very big problem. My dad was not going to lie to the court on my behalf. And the dude I bought the gun from sure as hell wasn't going to show up to act as a character witness.

"I just don't understand why you would do this," Mom said as we drove home.

"If you're waiting for me to change my story, it's not going to happen," I told her. "I'm not selling pot. I don't have any friends to sell it to. I wouldn't even know where to begin."

"I spoke with your principal."

"And? Am I suspended?"

Mom let out a sudden incredulous laugh that made me flinch.

"Suspended? You actually think you're only suspended? You've been *expelled*, Curtis."

"Expelled? For real?"

"Yes, for real. What did you think they were going to do?"

"So…so what happens next?"

"I don't know. I guess I have to quit my job so I can babysit my goddamn son all day. Then we have to figure out where to send you, assuming the court doesn't make that decision for us."

"What do you mean, figure out where to send me?"

"I don't know what that means yet. You got kicked out of school and you're too young to join the army, so we have some difficult goddamn decisions to make."

"Do you mean boarding school? What?"

"I mean exactly what I said. We don't know what we're going to do with you yet."

"It was Mr. Martin," I said. "Why won't you believe me?"

"You've been fixated on him since Todd disappeared. I get it. You think you saw Todd get into a car with him."

"I *think* I saw it?"

"They took your accusation seriously. They questioned him and searched his house. They've come back and questioned him again and again. I'm not saying he didn't do it. I'm saying that if they can't find enough evidence to arrest him for it, you need to let it go. Once you start accusing him of breaking into the house and planting drugs in your backpack, it's gone too far."

I just stared out the window for the rest of the car ride home.

Mom sent me to my room. I sat on my bed, listening to her crying downstairs.

Around noon she told me that lunch was ready. We sat at the dining room table, eating bologna sandwiches in silence. When we were done, I returned to my room.

I could fix this. I wasn't going to let Mr. Martin ruin my life. I wasn't going to go to a youth correctional facility because of him. He'd won this particular battle, but now I knew that I needed to step up my game.

When Dad got home from work, he didn't even come to check on me. I just heard him and Mom talking. It sounded like they were arguing, but I couldn't hear what they were saying.

The doorbell rang.

"Oh, hi," Dad said.

"Hi." It sounded like Tina's dad. "You know why I'm here, right?"

"I think so."

"I do not expect to see your son anywhere near Tina. Do you understand me? Nowhere near her. They will not be seeing each other, ever again, under any circumstances. If I see Curtis, I'll kill him. Do you hear me? Do I need to repeat it?"

"Okay, look, I know you're mad," Dad told him.

"You have no idea how mad I am."

"He will never see Tina again. I promise. But I can't stand here and let you threaten to kill him."

"You keep your drug-dealing kid away from my daughter and we won't have any problems."

"All right, all right. I'm going to have to ask you to leave now."

I heard the door close. A moment later, Dad walked into my room. "Don't call Tina ever again."

"I won't."

"I mean it."

"I said that I won't!"

Dad left, slamming my bedroom door behind him. Then he apparently decided that I should not be granted any privacy, because he opened it again, then walked away.

THE LAWYER, Mr. Nickles, wore a rumpled grey suit and looked frazzled. He adjusted his glasses and stroked his mustache as he looked at my file.

"Possession with intent to sell is a felony," he said. "You could be looking at up to five years' incarceration."

Mom, Dad, and I all gaped at him across the desk. "Are you serious?" Dad asked.

Mr. Nickles nodded. "It's unlikely, but we have to look at that as a worst-case scenario. Now, the possession part is pretty straightforward. He had a bag of pot in his backpack, which was found by a state trooper in the presence of the school principal. Curtis says it was planted there, but, surprise, *everybody* who's arrested on drug charges insists that they don't know how it got there."

"I know how it got there," I said.

"Quiet," Dad told me. "Let him talk."

"Intention to sell is a little harder to prove. If his backpack was filled with cash and the product was divided out into lots of small baggies, we'd know exactly what he meant to do with it. The fact that it was all in one bag helps his case. What does not help his case is that he had two ounces in there. That's when a judge starts to think, hmmm, maybe he's not just saving that for personal use. Getting caught with anything more than one ounce is very, very bad."

"What if—" I started to say, but Dad elbowed me in the side.

"Now, if you were an adult and you got busted with that much marijuana on school grounds, you'd be screwed. Fortunately, you're fourteen years old, and if you *were* intending to sell marijuana on school grounds, you were only intending to sell it to other fourteen-year-olds, and maybe some thirteen-year-olds. Still very bad, just not as bad as it could be. So let's discuss your options."

I leaned forward.

"Option one, you plead not guilty. It goes to trial. The guy you're accusing of planting the bag in your backpack will be questioned. Maybe he breaks down on the witness stand and confesses, but most likely he denies it. Ultimately, a jury is going to find it difficult to believe that a construction worker is breaking into somebody's home—or having a friend do it—to hide a fairly expensive bag of drugs in a teenager's belongings. I believe you, Curtis, and I'd do my best to make a jury believe it, but I'm telling you, it's a longshot. Same thing with intent to sell. Even if somebody could vouch for you being a complete pothead, two ounces is a lot of weed. That's a hundred and twenty joints, depending on how generously you roll them. Were you going to throw a huge party and give free pot to all your friends? Again, that's a longshot for a jury. If you've got more than an ounce, we automatically assume you're selling it. I'd do everything I could to make the jury see things your way, but I've got to be brutally honest, I'm seeing a guilty verdict here. You probably wouldn't get the five years. I can see one year in a juvenile detention center."

"Okay," I said, feeling like I'd been kicked in the stomach.

"What's option two?" Dad asked.

"Plead guilty. Try to work a deal where your incarceration time is nowhere close to a year. Maybe ninety days. Maybe only sixty. Maybe none at all—maybe I could set something up where you just get probation. That's not so bad. It just means that you're on your absolute best behavior at all times, and that you have to meet with a probation officer on a regular basis. Be ready for a surprise home inspection at any time."

Dad nodded. "What would that mean for college?"

"Well, I'm not a college admissions counselor. It wouldn't be ideal, obviously. His juvenile criminal record would be permanently sealed when he turned eighteen, so this wouldn't haunt him for the rest of his life."

"So you think it could just be probation?"

"It could be."

"When would we know?"

"The system doesn't move fast. Could be a few weeks. Could be a few months."

"Jesus."

"What's your suggestion?" Mom asked.

Mr. Nickles sighed. "I'd love to say that I could deliver a not-guilty verdict for your son. I'm simply not convinced of that. Maybe I can dissuade them of the idea that he was going to sell it, though that's not remotely a guarantee, but your son's backpack was in his possession the entire morning at school. Even if it wasn't, the idea that a fellow student had access to two ounces of marijuana that they could hide in there...you understand what I'm saying, right?"

"Yes," said Mom. "So your suggestion is to plead guilty."

"My suggestion is to wait to see what kind of deal I can work out. Again, it could just be probation. I assume Curtis was going to be on the straight and narrow from now on anyway—this just puts some extra eyes on him."

"Thank you," said Mom.

"Anytime."

"I DON'T WANT to plead guilty," I told my parents from the back of the car. "I didn't do anything wrong."

They ignored me.

IT's difficult to convey the sheer awfulness of the following weeks.

My mom took a month-long leave of absence from work, and I was assured that this was most definitely *not* good for our finances, especially now that I'd added lawyer fees. The concept of "fun" no longer existed in my world. No television. No time outside that wasn't carefully monitored as if I were already in prison. Mom had acquired some textbooks, and the only thing I did all day was study them until Mom yanked the book out of my hand and asked me questions about what I'd learned. I hadn't realized that being home-schooled involved being yelled at all the time.

I never wavered in my side of the story, but I also stopped actively pushing the "It was Mr Martin" narrative. It wasn't doing any good. Presumably the state troopers had questioned him about the marijuana, and he'd credibly denied any involvement. (Nobody was keeping me in the loop on what was happening with the serial killer, but for my own sanity I had to believe that they'd at least sent somebody over to ask him about it.)

One positive thing was that Mr. Martin and his friend hadn't broken into my house and tried to kill me and my family. I suppose that planting drugs in my backpack had been his next move, but he wouldn't take it further than that as long as I was a good little boy.

I didn't get to talk to Tina, of course. I wondered if she believed that Mr. Martin was the real culprit, or she thought she'd been sort-of dating a drug dealer. Again, for my own sanity I had to believe it was the former. If anything, I'd never offered her any weed.

Thanksgiving arrived. All of our extended family lived in the lower forty-eight, so Thanksgiving generally just involved the three of us, unless my parents invited friends over. I honestly thought that this year Mom would slap a turkey TV dinner on the table in front of me and say "Enjoy, asshole!" But, no, she went all-out as usual, with turkey, stuffing, mashed potatoes, cranberry sauce, rolls, and pumpkin pie.

We ate in uncomfortable silence. Nobody gave thanks for anything.

At the beginning of December, she had to either go back to work or officially quit her job. She decided that being my full-time captor wasn't how she wanted to spend her life, so she returned to her job at the bank but reinstated the policy that there would be frequent random calls, and I'd better answer immediately.

"I don't care if you're in the middle of taking a shit," she informed me. "You'd goddamn well better answer the phone when I call." Mom had taken up the use of profanity since discovering that her son was a criminal.

I goddamn well answered the phone every time she called. I was left each day with textbook reading assignments (Mom wouldn't prepare tests; she'd just look through the chapter and ask questions) and a gargantuan list of chores.

Throughout all this, of course, I had the ever-present worry that Mr. Martin *wasn't* satisfied with where he'd left things. I'd planned to wait until he let down his guard, and he might be planning the same thing. It would be stupid of him to try anything else—he had most definitely won this round—but that didn't mean he was done with me.

I also had the constant sick-to-my-stomach dread of how the plea bargain would go. What if Mr. Nickles said, "*Sorry, Curtis, there was nothing I could do. It's five years in juvie hall for you. As your lawyer, I'm advising you to kick somebody's ass the first day, or else your life will be a living hell and you'll always have to give up your dessert*"?

Wednesday, December 20th. Snow everywhere. Thirteen degrees below zero Fahrenheit. Twenty-five below Celsius. Cold.

Technically, the second-to-last day of autumn.

Mom, Dad, and I sat in Mr. Nickles' office. He let out a long, deep sigh.

"So…" he said.

We all stared at him expectantly.

"The lady who'll be prosecuting the case is a real hardass. I knew that, but I thought she'd be a little more reasonable than this. She acknowledges that her job is a lot harder because she hasn't identified any of your customers. But what she's saying, and I'm just the messenger here, is that a jury might think your friend's disappearance is related to the drugs."

Dad's eyes went wide and his face transformed into an expression of pure rage that quite honestly scared me. Mr. Nickles held up his hand, silencing Dad before he could start screaming at him.

"I would fight that. To me, it's irrelevant. It's not like Curtis was selling hard drugs. Still, her perspective is that he could be involved with non-law-abiding citizens, and the unsolved disappearance of his best buddy isn't going to help his case."

"So no plea bargain?" Mom asked.

"Oh, she offered a deal." He let out another long sigh. "Ninety days in a juvenile detention center, followed by two years of probation."

"Are you fucking joking?" Dad asked.

"That's the deal I was able to make. I hoped I could do better. I tried to get it down to sixty days but she wouldn't go for it. She thinks she'll win."

"And what do you think?"

"I don't think the 'best friend killed by drug dealers' angle is going to fly, but I also don't think a jury will believe that your son is innocent. I'm sorry, it's a harsh reality, yet that's the way it is. His incarceration would start after the new year. He'd still get to spend Christmas at home."

"Oh, well, that's a treat," I said.

"Shut up," Dad told me.

"All I can do is offer my advice," said Mr. Nickles. "Three months sounds terrible, and let's be honest, it *is* terrible, but if you're standing in front of the judge and he sentences you to five years, you'll wish you'd taken this deal. With good behavior, they'd probably release you before your sentence was up, instead of transferring you to a state prison when you turned eighteen."

Mom and Dad looked absolutely shellshocked.

"You can have some time to discuss it," Mr. Nickles said. "Not a lot of time—the deal expires today. You don't have to decide right this minute is what I mean."

"I'll take the deal," I told him, and then I began bawling.

Friday, December 21st. The last day of autumn.

Mr. Martin had fucked up.

If he wanted to get me off his back, his plan might have worked. Mr. Nickles could have offered me a year of probation, and it's entirely possible that I would have thought, *you know what, I need to just consider myself lucky that it wasn't worse, suck it up, and let this whole thing go.* I think Todd would have agreed that it was okay to let Mr. Martin get away with it, all things considered.

Instead, his plan worked too well. He'd deposited me firmly into the category of "What do I have to lose?"

During the drive home yesterday, I'd pretended to be contrite. Not to the point of lying and "admitting" that the marijuana was mine, but I tried to act very mature and say that I'd be on my absolute best behavior for the three months of incarceration, and then put all of this behind me. If they sent me to boarding school after my release, I'd be the best student that school had ever seen. This was the wake-up call I needed to turn my life around.

Basically, I needed Mom and Dad to feel comfortable going to work. I wanted them to know I wasn't suicidal. I wanted them to know I wasn't going to run away. I wanted them to *think* I was going to sit at home and try to enjoy my freedom before it was taken away.

When Mom suggested that maybe she should stay home, I said that it didn't matter to me either way. No suspicious "*No, no, no, you should go—I'll be fine!*"

She went to work. So did Dad.

Though I was feeling like I had nothing to lose, I knew that wasn't actually true, and I also didn't want to be a complete idiot. Showing up on school grounds would be disastrous. I assumed I was quite famous around there, and somebody would report me, which in turn would mean a call to my parents.

So I had to wait until school was over. Since this was a gigantic favor, I thought I needed to ask in person, not over the phone.

When I called a taxi, it was already dark. Fairbanks was down to less than four hours of daylight now.

After he picked me up, the cab driver asked why I wasn't in school. I said that I'd been expelled. He said, bummer, and that he could relate.

He dropped me off in front of Ed Loreen's house.

Hey, after our fight (or "fight") he'd said that if I needed anything, to let him know. I'd see if the bully actually meant it.

I stood there, shivering in the cold, hoping the address in the phone book had been correct. A few minutes later, the bus pulled up to the end of the street, and, yes, Ed got out. There were a few other kids with him, but they'd separated from him by the time he reached his driveway.

Ed grinned. "Hey, pothead, how's it going? Here to try to kick my ass again?"

"I could use your help."

"Come on inside. My parents won't be home for a couple of hours."

We went inside his house. Ed took off his too-light-for-the-cold-weather jacket and threw it on the living room floor. "I'm not going to make you hot chocolate or anything like that, so don't even ask."

"So I take it you heard about what happened to me?"

"Of course I did. Everybody did. You innocent?"

"Yeah."

"I believe you. You know why? Because I kept asking around to figure out who your customers were to see if they could hook me up, and nobody knew a damn thing about you selling weed. Are you here to sell me some?"

"No."

"Well, shit. What do you need?"

"I know who murdered Todd Lester. It's the same person who planted the drugs in my backpack. His name is Gerald Martin. He abducted and murdered at least four other kids. This summer I tried to force him to confess at gunpoint, and I was successful, but he got the gun away from me and threatened to kill my family if I said anything." Ed only needed the high-level explanation; this wasn't the time to get into the whole feeding tube threat. "Tonight I'm going to sneak out of my house, go over there, and force him to take me to where Todd's body is buried."

"I'm in," said Ed.

"You need to know the plan first. He's dangerous."

"Yeah, I recognize that the child-killer might be dangerous. What's your plan?"

"Can you pick a lock?" I asked.

"My older brother can. He'll pick a lock for you if I ask him to. And he's got a car. I'll bring Burt and Josh, too."

"I wasn't going to ask you or anybody else to confront him

directly. If your brother can help me break into his house, that saves me the trouble of stopping at the library to learn how to do it myself. Once I've got him, I wanted you to follow us to the burial site, and then help me dig."

"The ground will be frozen," said Ed.

"I know. That's why I'll need your help."

"Why don't you let him take you to the spot, and then call the police?"

"Because if he takes me to the wrong place, he can tell them he was bluffing to buy himself some time to be rescued. I need absolute proof first. Again, I'm not asking you to put yourself in danger. I'll take all the risks."

"I don't mind taking risks. How dangerous do you think that asshole will be if he's up against five of us?"

"I'm not sure," I said. "But, again, he's murdered several kids. He might have a gun."

"So will we."

"I honestly thought you'd be a lot more reluctant."

"Hell no. When am I gonna get another chance to kick the shit out of a madman? We've got your back, Curtis. Just tell me where we need to be."

THAT HAD GONE QUITE a bit better than I'd anticipated. After we finalized our plans, Ed let me use his phone to call another cab, and I was back on my way home. I had at least another hour before my mom got home from work, so as long as she hadn't called while I was gone, everything was going smoothly.

As we pulled up to my house, I could see that the lights were on.

Okay. Well, I'd known the risk. My attitude had been "What's she going to do, ground me?" If I'd known how receptive Ed would be to my plan, I probably would've called him instead.

I went inside, bracing myself for the firestorm.

"Where the hell were you?" Mom demanded. "Why didn't you answer the phone?"

I explained that I just wanted to go for a long walk to see the Christmas decorations. Ours was the only house that didn't have any. We also didn't have a Christmas tree or any presents. We used to put up the tree the day after Thanksgiving and cover the house with lights that could be seen from the edge of the earth's atmosphere, but the holidays had been cancelled in our household this year.

Mom yelled at me, then cried, then yelled some more, then went to her bedroom and slammed the door. I felt bad, but I couldn't just sit around anymore and await my fate. Maybe I'd clear my name. Maybe I'd spend the first three months of 1980 locked up. Maybe I'd be dead before the new year. However it worked out, the standoff between Mr. Martin and I was over.

When Dad got home, he yelled at me, and then he and Mom yelled at me together. I just sat there and took it. They asked if I *wanted* to be a juvenile delinquent, and I said no, I did not. They asked why I was behaving like this then, and I said that I didn't know. It was positively brutal.

They sent me to my room for a while.

We had flavorless meatloaf for dinner, then I went to bed.

I heard them arguing. Though it didn't devolve into shouting at each other, the arguing went on far longer than anything I'd ever heard from them.

Then they started watching television.

That was fine. It was only about ten o'clock. Even when they didn't have to go to work the next day, my parents were never up very late. I was supposed to meet Ed and the others at midnight.

An hour later, they were still watching television.

That was fine. I had plenty of time.

Now I could hear them arguing again.

I had to be outside at midnight. If I wasn't out there to meet him, Ed and his buddies weren't going to say, "Oh, hey, no problem. We'll just reschedule."

They turned off the television but continued to blame each other for the parenting failures that had led them to raise a drug-dealing liar.

Finally they stopped.

I'd wanted to give them more time to fall fast asleep, but I had to start getting ready. I wasn't sure what I'd do if they were awake when I needed to leave. I supposed I'd have to simply explain that I was going out whether they liked it or not, and assume that they wouldn't try to physically restrain me.

I left my bedroom and crept downstairs into the living room. A denim jacket wasn't going to cut it tonight. We might be outside for a long time, and it was *really* fucking cold out there, so impressing my peers was no longer a priority.

I opened the closet door as quietly as I possibly could.

I heard Mom say something from the bedroom, though I couldn't make out the actual words.

What was that other noise?

I stood there for a moment, trying to figure out what I was hearing.

Oh, Jesus Christ, my parents were having makeup sex.

The urge to slam my hands over my ears and sing "*I can't hear you la la la la la la la!*" was strong, but I focused on the task at hand and got my boots, a heavy jacket, gloves, a hat that I didn't like to wear because it itched, and a scarf out of the closet. I got dressed quickly and quietly, thankful that the noises were limited to moans and creaking bedsprings rather than graphic declarations. Technically, this was a rare moment of good luck, since if my parents were focused on carnal pleasure they were less likely to hear me sneak out of the house…but it was an element of trauma I really didn't need right before I headed out to face off against a serial killer.

I tiptoed into the kitchen, opened a drawer, and took out the same knife I'd brought the last time. Stuck it in my inside jacket pocket.

I went out through the back door.

Before visiting Ed, I'd taken a shovel out of the garage and left it by the back corner of the house, along with a flashlight. I'd also taken Dad's pistol out of the closet in his office, loaded it, and stashed it in the inside pocket of my jacket next to the knife. Yes, I would've preferred another untraceable gun, but I had to work with the options available to me.

I picked up the shovel, left my yard, and walked to the end of the block. I was a few minutes early, but a brown car with a cracked windshield, splotches of rust, and apparently no muffler was already there waiting for me.

The driver got out. I would've known he was Ed's older brother even if I'd run into him at the grocery or something—they looked almost exactly alike. He walked around to the back of the vehicle and opened the trunk. "I'm Mick," he said.

"I'm Curtis."

"Well, duh."

I put the shovel in the trunk, where it joined four others. There was also a gasoline can, several flashlights, some rope, and a rifle. I hadn't asked him to bring a rifle.

"Thanks for doing this," I said, shutting the trunk.

"Whoa, not so hard," Mick said. "You want to break it? This ain't a Rolls Royce."

"Sorry."

"Get in before we both freeze to death."

I opened the back door. There were already three people sitting there. Ed's buddies Burt and Josh, and between them, Tina.

"Tina!" I said, because sometimes you say unnecessary things out loud.

"Get in and close the door," said Ed from the front seat. "You're letting in cold air."

"I'm not sure there's room," I said.

"Everybody scoot over. No, let Tina sit on his lap."

Burt got out of the car, followed by Tina, and then Burt got back in while Tina gave me a tight hug. "I'm sorry," she said. "There was no way my dad would've let me call you."

"Get in the goddamn car," said Ed.

I got in, and Tina sat on my lap. We closed the door.

"Where to?" Mick asked.

I gave him directions to Mr. Martin's house.

"You surprised?" Ed asked me. "I figured you'd want the chance to see your girlfriend again."

I had conflicting emotions about it. I was thrilled to see her again, and I was not opposed to having her sit on my lap, but we weren't on our way to a party. This could get bloody.

"I told my dad I was spending the night at a friend's house," said Tina. "Since I haven't talked to you in almost two months, he didn't think anything was weird about it."

"Ed told you what we're doing, right?" I asked.

"Yes. I know it's dangerous. But you need help."

We drove into Mr. Martin's subdivision. A few houses away, I told Mick to stop. He parked on the side of the street and shut off the headlights.

"It's just going to be me, Mick, and Ed for right now," I explained. Mick was going to pick the lock. Ed was going to hold the flashlight for him. And I was going to keep watch.

The three of us got out of the car and retrieved a couple of flashlights from the trunk.

Then we walked toward Mr. Martin's house.

19

It was after midnight. There'd been snow since October, but winter had officially begun.

The Northern Lights were out in full force, displaying beautiful green streaks across the night sky. Nobody ever got used to them. You didn't look up at the Aurora Borealis, shrug, and say "Eh, seen it." Even now, I took a few seconds to admire them, before turning my attention to the extremely unpleasant task ahead.

We quietly walked up Mr. Martin's driveway and around to the back of his house. Mick, armed with a straightened-out paper clip, began to work on picking the lock to his back door. Ed held the flashlight beam on the doorknob. I stood there and wondered what the hell I was doing here.

This could go so horribly wrong, and I could drag others down with me.

"Hurry up," Ed whispered.

"Shut up," Mick told him. "I'm trying to concentrate."

"You said you could do this."

"I didn't say I could do it fast."

"It's okay," I quietly assured both of them. "We're not in a hurry."

We *were* in a hurry, of course. Every extra second we were out here carried the risk of getting caught. But I didn't want them to keep bickering, and I didn't want Mick to get flustered. We'd be fine.

"Hurry the fuck up," Ed whispered, ten minutes later.

"Kiss my ass," said Mick.

"No, because my lips would freeze to it. Can you pick the lock or not?"

"It's not the kind of lock I thought it would be. And it's cold."

"What does it being cold have to do with anything?"

"Metal contracts in the cold."

"Oh, for fuck's sake."

"Guys, you're being too loud," I warned. "Do you think you'll be able to pick it?"

"I will if he shuts the fuck up," said Mick.

"I've been shutting the fuck up for half an hour now."

"It's been five minutes."

"It's been ten minutes," I said. "It's not a big deal. Just keep working."

"Here, give me the paper clip," said Ed, twenty minutes after we'd arrived at Mr. Martin's back door.

"How about I shove the paper clip up your ass?"

"How about you bite my dick?"

"How about you bite *my* dick?"

"I really need you guys to knock it off," I said. Then I realized that we weren't alone out here.

A great big moose was walking through Mr. Martin's backyard.

This wasn't entirely unheard of. Alaska was chock full of moose, and, yes, on rare occasions they would walk through your yard even in a neighborhood like this.

"There's a moose over there," said Mick.

"Ignore the moose," said Ed. "Worry about the lock."

"But it's *right there.*"

"I see the fucking moose. What I don't see is an open door."

The moose stopped walking and turned to look at us.

"Hi, Moose," said Mick, waving to it. I honestly was starting to wonder if Ed had told his brother the full story of why we were here. Maybe Mick thought we were breaking into Mr. Martin's house to steal something.

We all watched the moose for a moment.

Then it continued on its way.

Ed punched Mick in the shoulder. "Get back to work."

"Don't punch him so hard," I said. "We're trying to be quiet."

"You think I won't stop what I'm doing and kick your ass?" Mick asked Ed.

"As far as I can tell, you're not doing anything."

"I'll kick your ass, and then you can walk home."

"Oh, yeah, Mom will love that. Let me die like that kid who just froze to death."

"I'll do it. You can be a fuckin' popsicle for all I care."

"This was a bad idea," I said. "We should leave." If we were here much longer, Burt, Josh, and Tina might come check on us, and we'd wake up Mr. Martin for sure.

"No, wait, I've almost got it," said Mick.

"Bullshit," said Ed.

"I've almost got it if you quit moving the flashlight."

Ed held the flashlight steady. Mick twisted the paper clip around a few more times, and then there was a click.

"See? No problem at all."

I wasn't sure if I was relieved or disappointed. I really didn't want to go in there, but I also didn't want to spend three months in kid-prison.

"Thanks," I told Mick. "Go back to the car and let the others know that everything's fine. Ed, you wait here while I go in."

"I'll come in with you."

I shook my head. "I'm not going to get you killed."

"Teamwork, man."

"Stay outside."

"Whatever."

I very slowly opened the back door, half-expecting a blaring alarm to go off, waking up Mr. Martin and everybody on his block. It didn't happen. I stepped inside, and then very slowly closed the door again, not shutting it all the way to keep the noise level to a minimum.

I was in his garage. It was an extremely tidy garage—almost creepily so. His car was parked inside, so he was definitely home. I walked over to the door that led to the interior of the house, thinking that if it was locked, I might have to just abandon discretion and try to kick it open.

I took off the itchy hat and shoved it into my pocket. I hated that thing.

The door was unlocked. I opened it and stepped into his kitchen.

I walked through his living room and into a dark hallway.

The door at the end was open, revealing the bathroom. There was a door to the left and the right. Both were closed.

I unzipped my jacket, reached inside, and took out the gun.

After a few moments to consider my decision—a waste of time, since I had absolutely no information to help me decide which door might be the correct one—I chose the door to the left. Should I fling it open, or try to be quiet? I decided that if I picked the wrong door, I'd wish I'd been quieter about it, so I carefully turned the knob, then slowly pushed it open.

I flipped on the light switch.

It was an office. A couple of bookshelves, a desk, and some neatly stacked cardboard boxes.

I shut off the light and returned to the hallway.

I pressed my ear to the other door, trying to hear Mr. Martin snoring.

Nothing.

Burst in, or try to open it without waking him up?

I'd stick with trying to be sneaky for now. If I heard any sign of movement, I'd burst in.

I turned the doorknob as slowly as I could. I realized that my breathing was way too loud and tried to keep that under control. Could a fourteen-year-old have a heart attack? If they could, I was headed for that fate. I'd point the gun at him, clutch my chest, and collapse to the floor.

I pushed on the door. It didn't creak. In fact, it made no sound at all, so my bravery increased and I pushed it open all the way.

I flipped on the light.

This was Mr. Martin's bedroom. But he wasn't there. The bed was unmade.

Where was he? Surely he hadn't gone for an after-midnight walk in sub-zero weather.

Had he heard me walking around? Had he heard us picking the lock? Was he hiding somewhere in the house?

Shit.

It felt like making a beeline for the back door and getting the hell out of there might be the best course of action. Except that if Mr. Martin knew I'd broken into his home, he wouldn't simply say, "Oh, well, he left on his own, so there's no need to pursue this matter further." It was more important than ever that I follow through with the plan.

I peeked under his bed. Nothing. I opened the closet door, ready for him to pop out with a butcher knife. He didn't.

He wasn't in the office.

Wasn't hiding in the bathroom behind the shower curtain.

I walked back into the living room. He wasn't there.

Wasn't in the kitchen.

I hadn't actually looked inside of his car. He might've been lying in the back seat, but if you heard kids trying to pick the lock to break into your house, would you really hide in your car?

If he *was* in the house, I was pretty sure he was down in the basement.

I didn't want to descend into the basement. But I had no choice. Too bad for me.

I went back into the kitchen. I hadn't noticed it before, but the door that I assumed led to the basement was ajar. I very, very, very slowly opened it wide enough for me to get through, then took one step down.

There was a light on down there. Not a bright one—probably just a small lamp.

I took another step down.

I could hear something.

I took one more step down, which was as far as I could go before my feet became visible. I listened carefully.

Mr. Martin was talking to somebody.

"I know, I know," he said. "Sometimes it's just so hard. You know what I mean? I feel like I'm burning up inside. Have you heard of spontaneous human combustion? It's when you burst into flames. Your whole body gets consumed by fire and turns to ashes, but it doesn't mess with the things around you. You could be sitting on a wooden chair and they'll just find your ashes on it. Not a mark on the wood. I'm not saying I believe in this—I don't—it's just how I feel, like I'm going to burst into flame."

Nobody else spoke. He was either talking on the telephone or talking to himself.

"I'm not going to," he said. "I want to but I'm not going to. It would be stupid. I think about it all the time, though. When I'm on the job, swinging a hammer or something, you'd better believe that I'm fantasizing about it." He laughed, then sniffled. "Nah, if I do that I'll just lie awake. I haven't had a good night's sleep in I don't know how long. It's like I see stuff moving around on the ceiling. I can't tell if I'm awake or in the middle of a nightmare. I can't wait to be able to move away from here. Start over. Maybe a big city. The kind where kids disappear all the time. I don't want to get help. Stop saying that."

I didn't know the optimal moment to reveal myself. It was unlikely that I'd be fortunate enough to find him looking in the other direction, allowing me to sneak right up on him, so it might be best to do it while he was engaged in a phone conversation. But I also didn't want him to shout for the person on the other end to call the police.

"Hold on," he said.

I stopped breathing.

"Hello?" he called out.

I just stood there, feeling like he could hear my heart pounding.

He was silent for a moment.

"I'm not sure," he said. "Paranoia, probably. But I'm entitled, right? Hey, I just want you to know that I really appreciate you talking to me like this. Helps keep me sane. Without an outlet, things would be a lot worse than they are. Yeah, yeah, I know you're happy to do it, but you still have better things you could be doing. Like sleeping. What time is it? I don't even know. Oh, okay, that's earlier than I thought."

I had to make my move. I couldn't creep down the stairs, because if he was facing that direction, I didn't want him to watch me slowly descend and have time to retrieve his trusty axe. This pretty much had to be a "Surprise!" moment, though I would not actually shout that.

I hurried down the stairs, making sure the gun in my hand was clearly visible.

Mr. Martin had a fully furnished basement, like a downstairs living room. It was actually cozier looking than his upstairs. He was seated on a recliner, legs up, a blanket on his lap, a few empty bottles of beer on the side table next to him. He held a black telephone receiver to his ear.

"You know what, I have to go," Mr. Martin said into the phone. "Tell Mom I love her."

He placed the receiver back on its cradle.

"Toss the blanket away," I said. "Do it with one hand."

Mr. Martin tossed the blanket to the floor. He was wearing the same robe as when I'd bothered him on Halloween.

"Lower your feet."

He pulled the handle on the side of the recliner, lowering the footrest.

"Can I get you a beer?" he asked.

"Stand up," I told him.

"Jeez, you're pretty bossy tonight."

"I said, stand up."

196

Mr. Martin stood up. "Anything else I can do for you? Want me to get down on my knees and put my hands behind my head? Make it nice and easy for you to execute me?"

"What you can do for me is stop talking unless I ask you a question."

Mr. Martin put his hand to his chin, as if giving deep contemplation to what I'd said. "Hmmm. Are you the kind of person who would murder me for talking? I'm not sure. You do look pretty angry right now, but I think that deep inside, your heart is in the right place. I think I can talk without you killing me. I guess I'll find out, huh?"

"I bet you'd sober up if I shot you in the leg," I said.

"Oh, yeah. Alcohol would spray out of the bullet hole instead of blood. Why are you here, Curtis? If you're here to kill me, kill me. Blow my head off and get it over with. Or shoot my eyes out." He tapped his right eye with his index finger. "Bring the barrel of your gun right up here and pull the trigger."

I said nothing. He lowered his hand. After a moment of silence, his shoulders slumped and he looked truly, deeply sad.

"Why are you here?" he asked.

"You're taking me to Todd's body."

"No, I'm not."

"I didn't ask if you *would* take me to his body. I said that you *are* taking me to his body.

"I buried it."

"I know. You already told me that."

"Did I really?"

"Yes. You said that if my last words impressed you, you'd bury me next to him."

"I don't remember that."

"I do."

"I won't be able to find it again."

197

"That's a lie."

"It's out in the woods. There's no way I'll be able to take you to the exact spot."

"I think you can. You'll have the right motivation."

"So, what, you're going to kill me if I can't find it?"

I shook my head. "Not finding it isn't an option. I'm going to torture you until you *do* find it."

"Like how?"

"It'll be a surprise."

"I buried him in the summer. It's freezing out there now. We'd have to wade through a mile of snow—probably up to our waist. It's pitch black out. It'll never work."

"You'll make it work. What do you think I've been doing all this time?" I asked. "Take a guess. What do you think I've been doing since the day I saw you drive away with my best friend? Go on, answer the question."

"No clue."

"I've been fantasizing about torturing you. I've got *months'* worth of dark shit in my head that I'm ready to let out if you don't cooperate."

Mr. Martin smiled. "You think I'm scared of you?"

"You should be."

"Nah. That's not the way this works. You way overestimate how worried I am about some lard-ass brat who can't even hold a gun right."

He took a step toward me.

"Don't move," I warned.

"Or what? You'll drop the gun and run away? Kid, you're a great big pain in the butt, but that's as far as it goes. You're not an actual threat to me. If you're looking for somebody to be trembling in fear, you need to look someplace else."

He took another step toward me, this one cartoonishly slow and exaggerated.

"I told you not to move."

"And yet I keep moving."

"Don't make me shoot you."

"Aw, you're just adorable," said Mr. Martin, as he walked toward me.

20

I wasn't bluffing.

I aimed the pistol at his leg and squeezed the trigger. This whole process would be much more difficult if he was wounded, but I had no choice. Burt and Josh could drag him through the snow, if necessary.

The gun didn't fire.

I squeezed the trigger again. Nothing.

Was the safety on? I flipped it off with my thumb and tried again. Now the trigger wouldn't budge. The safety had been off before, and now I'd turned it on. I flipped the switch again and squeezed the trigger once more. Absolutely nothing happened.

The gun was definitely loaded. I obviously hadn't had a chance to test it before I got here, but I was almost positive I'd loaded it correctly. What the hell was wrong with it? My dad never went hunting and rarely went out for target practice, so the gun hadn't been fired in a long time, but still—

I swung the gun at Mr. Martin's face. If I couldn't shoot him, I could at least break his nose with it.

He blocked the swing. He dug his fingernails into my wrist. Construction workers in the late 1970's did not tend to have long fingernails, so he didn't draw blood, but it hurt enough to make me wince in pain.

He wrenched the gun out of my hand and pointed it at my face.

My hands immediately went up to cover my face, instinctively, as if that would help. *"Good thing his hands were up there to deflect the bullet when he got shot in between the eyes. Otherwise it would've been messy!"*

He squeezed the trigger. Nothing happened. He tried again with the same result.

Mr. Martin let out a snort of laughter. "What a piece of crap," he said, tossing the gun away.

Then he punched me in the mouth.

I stumbled backwards, arms pinwheeling, desperately trying to keep my balance. But "maintaining balance" was not one of my strongest skill sets, and I fell on my ass. Blood dribbled down my chin from my newly split lip.

Though I'd envisioned many different scenarios for how this could play out, I hadn't really thought about it becoming a fistfight. If that was the case, I was going to lose.

"Get up," Mr. Martin told me.

I tried.

"Actually, no. Stay down." He kicked me in the stomach. Had he not been wearing slippers, and I not been wearing a heavy jacket, that would've been the end of our battle. Still, he got me directly in the gut and it hurt. I clutched my stomach with one hand and gasped for breath, while I reached into my inside jacket pocket with my other hand.

"I have to kill you," said Mr. Martin. "You know that, right? If you'd left well enough alone, we could've enjoyed our little truce, and I eventually would've moved away and been some other shithead kid's problem. But now I can't let you walk out of here. I have to kill you and get out of town. We both lose."

"Sorry," I said.

"I didn't spend a lot of time with Todd, but he seemed kind of pathetic. His death was no big loss to the world. I'm sure you could've made new friends. Why squander everything for that ugly little fuck? The fact that I was able to fool him into getting in my car is proof enough that he didn't deserve to live. I took him out of the gene pool."

He was clearly trying to make me angry, but I wasn't sure what strategy he was employing. I was lying on the floor, crumpled in pain. Did he think that by filling me with rage he'd trick me into making *another* mistake? Most likely, he was just drunk and not thinking about what he was saying.

"If I had a knife down here, I'd slit your throat," he said. "Want to be a good boy and wait while I go upstairs and get one?"

"Sure."

"Oh, you'd like that, wouldn't you?" he asked, sneering as if he thought that I'd truly believed he was going to do that. "How about I just stomp your head into chunky slime? No, my boots are upstairs. I bet I can break your neck in three or four kicks, though. I'm not even wearing shoes and I can snap your neck with a few kicks. Let's try it."

As he swung his foot back, preparing for a vicious kick, I pulled out the knife.

I lunged at him with the knife as he tried to kick me.

In a perfect world, the blade would have sunk deep into the bottom of his foot, soaking his slipper with blood. Perhaps the blade would have gone all the way through, popping out through the top of his foot. Mr. Martin would gape at it in shock and horror for a moment, and then let out a shriek of agony.

What actually happened is that he saw the knife just as he started the kick, so he stopped it in progress and did an awkward couple of hops backwards. I sat up and swung the knife at him, missing by so much that I'm not sure why I even bothered to take the swing.

"Oh, had a trick up your sleeve, huh?" Mr. Martin asked. He cracked his knuckles. "Things are getting interesting."

I stood up. Despite having spent all that time outside in the cold, I was now starting to sweat. I pointed the knife at him. "Don't make me use this," I said. It sounded a lot more threatening in my head than when I said it out loud.

"I'm coming after you," said Mr. Martin. "So when you use that knife, you'd better make it count. You'd better jam it into my throat or plunge it straight into my heart. If you just stab me in the arm or stick it in my side, that won't be enough."

I could scream for help.

If Ed came down, it would be two against one. And Ed was one of the biggest kids in school. Together we could beat him.

Probably.

But what if I got him killed? What if I had to watch while Mr. Martin twisted Ed's neck until it snapped?

I couldn't do it. And I couldn't shout for him to call the police. Without evidence—such as the corpse of Todd Lester, recovered from its shallow grave—I was just some lunatic kid who'd broken into a man's house and threatened him with a knife. I'd get more than three months in juvie for that.

I sure as hell didn't want to *die,* but I couldn't be responsible for other deaths.

"I have a backup plan," I told him.

"I assumed you did from the very beginning. I don't give a shit."

I wiped some blood off my mouth and chin. There was more of it than I'd realized.

And then, without warning, I charged at him with the knife.

"Without warning" was the intention, anyway. I did not move with ninja-like prowess. He had enough time to brace himself for the attack. He stepped out of the way at the last instant and smacked me in the side of the head so hard that my ears started ringing and I thought he might have burst an eardrum.

He grabbed my jacket by the hood and yanked it. My head jerked backward. Then he shoved me forward, and I careened into a table, knocking over a lamp as I crashed to the floor.

Even with the padding, I hurt all over. This wasn't like a movie. In real life, smashing into a table like this would mean a trip to the emergency room. It would ruin my entire day. But lying there in pain feeling sorry for myself was not an option if I wanted to still be alive a couple of minutes from now. I picked up the knife that I hadn't realized that I'd dropped and forced myself to get up.

Mr. Martin had picked up one of his beer bottles.

He flung it at me, hitting me in the chest.

He grabbed another one and threw it. I'm not sure exactly where he was aiming, but if he'd been aiming for my funny bone on my right arm, his aim was perfect. My arm went numb and I dropped the knife again.

He picked up a third bottle. Now that I didn't have a weapon, there was no need for him to throw it. He walked over to me with long strides and smashed the bottle against my head, shattering the glass.

Though I knew that it wouldn't feel *good*, I could never have imagined how badly this would hurt. I was instantly dizzy. Blood streamed down my face.

Yet somehow I didn't fall over.

There was a lot of blood dripping onto my jacket with a pattering sound, but I had to stay calm. Head wounds bled a lot.

That was simply how it worked. It wasn't as if he'd slashed open an artery or anything.

I realized that he was still holding the neck of the bottle.

He slammed the jagged glass into my chest.

It didn't pierce my jacket.

He slammed it again, even harder.

My jacket still protected me.

With his third attempt, the glass went through my jacket and pierced my skin.

I punched him in the jaw. It was an accurate punch, and a surprisingly hard one; unfortunately, I was still wearing my gloves. This time, the padding worked against me instead of in my favor. It had an impact, but he didn't drop to the floor unconscious.

My left eye started to burn as blood trickled into it.

He slammed the broken bottle into my chest again, then grabbed my jacket with both hands and threw me across the room. I smashed into a record player, knocking it off its stand and also spilling twenty or thirty vinyl records onto the floor.

I stopped myself from falling by grabbing his recliner. There was a big spatter of blood where I'd hit the wall. I couldn't see out of my left eye now.

This should have been the part where I regretted coming here. It had been a horrible mistake. I was going to die. I hadn't done a goddamn thing to avenge Todd's murder. If we met in the afterlife, he'd say, "*Thanks for nothing, loser.*"

But I didn't regret it.

Because even though my whole body ached and my eye stung from the blood in it and I was scared and I quite honestly wanted to call out for my Mom and Dad, I was also so angry that I felt like I could tear off his head with my bare hands. Just rip it right the hell off and squash it between my gloved palms.

For four months, this son of a bitch hadn't allowed me to have a moment of genuine peace. He was always lurking in my mind, keeping me from focusing on my schoolwork, keeping me from having a normal relationship with my girlfriend, trying to put a huge black mark on my future.

I was done with him. This ended tonight. And I was going to win.

I let out a cry of fury—which wasn't my intent; it just happened —and ran at him.

His eyes widened in surprise. I guess he thought I was ready to just give up.

I tackled him.

I had rage, adrenaline, and determination on my side...yet I was still a chubby non-athletic teenager who was up against a serial killer who did manual labor all day. My attack elicited a grunt as I collided with him, but had no real impact. He shoved me against the wall again, adding a new spatter of blood to his décor. Then he strode toward me.

I frantically looked around for something I could use as a weapon.

There was plenty of stuff, but he got there before I could grab anything.

He smashed me into the wall. The back of my head struck the wood paneling and my vision went black for an instant.

He did it again.

And again.

"You really thought you were going to beat me?" Mr. Martin asked. He ran his finger across my forehead, held it up so I could see the blood, then wiped it under my nose. "Gave you a blood mustache," he said. "You're too young to grow anything but peach fuzz, and you seriously thought you were going to win?"

He smashed me into the wall once more.

"That wasn't hypothetical," he said. "That was a real question. Did you really think you were going to win?"

"Yes," I said. Some flecks of blood sprayed from my mouth onto his face when I said it.

"You're an idiot. You could've made some new friends in the slammer. Now I have to beat you to death. I'm going to beat you until you're *muck*, Curtis. Muck. Sludge. But I may take some parts with me as souvenirs. Maybe your heart and one of your arms. I didn't keep any parts of Todd or the others, and I always kind of regretted it. I won't make that mistake again."

I spat some blood in his face, this time on purpose.

He smashed me against the wall yet again.

"Let him go," said Tina.

Mr. Martin and I both glanced over at the stairs. Tina was walking down them, followed by Ed, Mick, Burt, and Josh. They all had shovels, and they looked ready to beat somebody to death with them.

Mr. Martin looked back at me, then back at them, then back at me.

He wiped off the blood I'd spit in his face.

Stepped away from me.

My legs began to buckle but I forced myself to remain upright.

"You kids better get off my property," he said. "You're trespassing."

"Are you okay?" Tina asked me.

I nodded. "Yeah, I'm fine." Then I winced as blood ran into my right eye as well. I kept it open because blindness would be extremely inconvenient right now, but it burned like crazy.

All five of them walked down the stairs into the basement. Mr. Martin was starting to look twitchy, as if he wanted nothing more than to engage in wholesale slaughter but knew he couldn't beat five shovel-wielding teenagers.

"I'll call the police," he said. "I've done nothing wrong." He pointed to me. "He broke into my house. I'm within my rights to defend myself. You'll all go to jail. Every one of you needs to walk right back up those stairs and get the hell out of my house."

"No," said Tina. "We won't be doing that."

"So what are you going to do?" Mr. Martin asked. "Beat me to death?"

"I already told you the plan," I said. "It hasn't changed."

"Refresh my memory."

"You're taking us to Todd's body."

"And I told you that was impossible."

"And I told you that I don't believe you."

Mr. Martin shrugged. "I can't find it again. If you want to kill me, kill me, but there's nothing I can do."

"We're not going to kill you," I said. "I'm just going to let them shatter your hands."

I wished I'd said this in a more sinister and descriptive manner. *"I'm going to let each of them shatter one finger in turn, starting with your pinky. Don't make the mistake of believing that they're going to do it quickly and efficiently. They're going to use the tips of their shovels and crush your poor fingers until they're—what's the word you used?— muck. Sludge. And when they're finally done, and you're gaping in horror at the bloody mess that used to be your left hand, I'll ask you again to take me to Todd Lester's burial place. And I'll expect a different answer. Now, Mr. Martin, do we understand each other?"* But I was lucky I could talk at all. My version was abbreviated but coherent.

"Let me shatter his hands anyway," said Ed. I wasn't sure if he was playing along or if the request was legitimate. For my own peace of mind, I decided that he was just playing along.

"All right," said Mr. Martin. "I'll do what I can. I can't make any promises."

"That's a better answer," I said. "But it's still not the right answer. You *are* taking us to Todd's body, and it's going to get worse and worse for you the longer it takes. If you think you can wait us out, take us to the wrong spots until we give up, you're wrong."

I saw something in Mr. Martin's expression I'd never seen before. He looked *defeated*.

"All right," he said. "Can I at least dress for the weather?"

21

I figured that four kids with shovels was enough to guard Mr. Martin while he put on his winter clothing, so I let Tina take me into the bathroom to clean up the blood and apply some bandages.

"You're going to need stitches," she informed me.

"Sorry, you know I love you but I'm not letting you stitch me up," I said.

Had I actually said, "I love you?" Jesus Christ. The timing was awful and I'd said it in a way that would have her wondering if I was being sarcastic. Our focus should be on Mr. Martin, not emotional confusion. Having a bottle shattered over my head was apparently not good for my brain function.

Tina ran some water in the sink. Apparently her reaction was going to be "ignore the comment." I approved of this reaction.

She held a washcloth under the tap and used it to wipe the blood off my face. She had to rinse it about six times before she declared it "good enough." I could see out of both eyes now, at least.

"You should've been wearing your hat," she said.

"It itches."

"So get one that doesn't itch."

"I will."

She applied what seemed to be a dozen bandages to my face. "You're swelling up pretty bad. When we get outside you should break off an icicle or something and hold it on there."

"Let me see," I said, reaching for the medicine cabinet door.

Tina closed the cabinet. "No. It's grotesque. It'll upset you."

"Now my imagination will make it worse."

"You're not horribly disfigured," she assured me. "You just look like somebody beat you up. For a few hours."

"Thanks for saving me," I said.

"Mick told us everything was fine, and we all kind of decided that we should go over and wait outside the house in case things stopped being fine. Good thing you guys were making a lot of noise."

"Yeah, I tried to make sure my bones broke as loudly as possible."

"You don't have any broken bones."

"I'm surprised."

"I don't know what to do about the top of your head," said Tina. "I can't really stick bandages to it because of your hair. I think I just need to stick a bunch of gauze on it as best that I can, and then you'll have to wear the itchy hat."

A minute later we walked out of the bathroom. Mr. Martin was dressed in a parka (that Ed had thoroughly searched) and snow pants. His look of defeat was gone. Now he looked like, given the opportunity, he would try to murder me with his teeth.

"It's time to go," I announced.

THERE WERE ONLY two licensed drivers among us, and we didn't think it would be a good idea for Mr. Martin to drive, even if we had a knife pressed against his side. We decided that Mick would drive Mr. Martin's car, with Tina riding in the front seat. I'd sit in the back, next to Mr. Martin with his wrists and feet tied together.

Ed had his learner's permit, so he was going to drive Mick's car, with Burt and Josh as passengers, and hope that he didn't get pulled over for any reason. Of course, we'd have a tied-up guy with us, so we didn't want to get pulled over, either. We'd obey all traffic laws.

"Don't go into the ditch," Mick told Ed.

"I won't."

"People go into the ditch all the time. Don't be one of them."

"I won't."

"Don't hit a moose."

"I won't. Shut the fuck up."

We led Mr. Martin into the garage, then Burt, who claimed to be the best at knots, tied up his hands and feet. We got him into the back seat and shut the door. Ed, Burt, and Josh headed back to Mick's car.

I went around and got into the back seat. I showed Mr. Martin my knife. "Don't make me slam this into your leg."

He turned away from me and didn't say anything.

Mick got in the car and started the engine. Tina pressed the button to raise the garage door. After Mick backed the vehicle out, she pressed the button again to close it, then climbed into the front seat and fastened her seat belt.

We pulled up alongside the car with Ed and his friends.

"Tell us where to go," I told Mr. Martin.

"Go straight," he muttered.

We drove off, with Ed following closely behind.

Mr. Martin gave us directions one turn at a time, but otherwise said nothing. No taunting, no threats, no pleading...he just sat there. I kept my guard up the entire time. If I lost focus for a second, that could be enough. I doubted there was anything he could do to me with his hands and feet tied together, but thinking, "*Oh, I'm perfectly safe!*" would surely lead to disaster.

We drove for about forty-five minutes, mostly on Chena Hot Springs Road, a long paved road with woods on each side that led us out of Fairbanks. I was sitting sideways, facing Mr. Martin, so I could see the headlights behind us in my peripheral vision. I kept waiting for Ed to careen off the road, in which case we'd have to go with Plan B, which involved squeezing the other three kids into Mr. Martin's car. Plan B would suck.

"Slow down," said Mr. Martin. "We should be coming up on the next turn. I'm not positive."

"Ptarmigan Pass?" asked Mick.

"Yeah, that's it."

Mick slowed way down, then turned left onto a dirt road. It had been plowed recently but there was a layer of new snow that hopefully wouldn't cause problems for Ed.

A moment later, Ed fishtailed and went off the road.

Mick stopped and cursed.

This would have been a perfect time for Mr. Martin to use our distraction to his advantage, so I refused to stare out the back windshield. Tina opened her door and got out. She hurried back to investigate, then quickly returned.

"They're completely off the road," she said. "It'll take a tow truck to get them out."

Ed sat in the passenger seat with Tina on his lap. I was squeezed tightly against Mr. Martin, with Burt and Josh also packed into a back seat that most definitely was not intended to accommodate four people. I could barely move, and my hands and feet were free, so I had to assume that Mr. Martin posed no danger unless he decided to try to bite a chunk out of my neck.

All of the shovels and flashlights were now in the trunk of Mr. Martin's car.

"You dumbass," said Mick.

"It wasn't my fault," Ed insisted.

"You were driving."

"The wheels just spun out of control. What was I supposed to do? Levitate the car?"

"You're paying for the tow truck."

"I'm not paying for shit. Curtis can pay for it. We're out here because of him."

"I'll pay for it," I said. "How much further?" I asked Mr. Martin.

"I'm not sure."

"Give us an estimate."

"About a mile."

The road split off every once in a while, but we kept on the main path until a mile and a half later.

"There," said Mr. Martin. "Take a right."

"There's no road there," said Mick.

"Yes, there is."

"It hasn't been plowed."

"That's not my problem. I said this was going to be impossible."

Mick stopped the car and looked back at me. "What now?"

"I guess we walk. We knew this was going to be a bitch."

Everybody got out of the car except for me and Mr. Martin. I waited for the others to distribute the shovels and flashlights. Instead of a shovel, Burt had a gasoline can. Josh had a snow shovel, while the others had one for digging in the dirt.

"Don't try to screw me over," I told Mr. Martin.

He glared at me. "You've already made that point."

"If I get the sense that you're jerking me around, or trying to lead us into some kind of trap, even if I'm wrong, it will be *horrible* for you. Those guys are psychopaths. They would love nothing more than for me to give them the go-ahead to fuck you up. The whole reason they're helping me is because they hope you screw up."

"And the fact that I've said over and over that I'm not going to be able to find the grave doesn't mean anything to you?"

"Nope. It sure doesn't."

I slid out of the car on the other side, then went around to open the door for Mr. Martin. We'd lose a lot of time if I made him hop through the snow, so as he swung his legs out of the vehicle I cut the rope binding his feet.

He held out his hands.

"Sorry," I said. "Your hands stay tied."

"What if I fall?"

"Then we'll pick you up."

He got out of the car. "This will be a lot easier if I can hold a flashlight myself instead of just telling you where to point one."

"That's a good point," I said. "But fuck you."

Mr. Martin shrugged.

"Every person here has permission to bash you with their shovel if you get out of line," I informed him.

"Noted."

"How far do we have to walk?"

"Far."

THE SNOW in the woods was not quite waist-deep, but it was above our knees, and trekking through it was absolutely miserable. I couldn't remember ever having been so cold. Slush was leaking into my boots and my feet were going numb. I couldn't feel my face, though I supposed that was a good thing.

It was possible that Mr. Martin was telling the truth; that he literally would not be able to find the spot where he buried Todd. He would have done the deed in daylight—even if he did it at midnight—and without snow on the ground. Yet I had to believe that if you murdered a boy and buried him in the woods, you'd remember where you did it. Even if it wasn't seared into your memory, you'd want to find your way back in case you heard that the area was being searched.

Or maybe not. Maybe you'd want to hide him where nobody, including yourself, could ever find him again. I was trying to guess the thought process of a diseased mind. I at least assumed that there was only so far into the woods that you'd take a corpse. You weren't going to hike for ten miles dragging a dead teenager behind you.

It honestly felt like we'd been walking for ten miles, but I doubted it was even a full mile yet. To their credit, nobody had asked to turn back and nobody was complaining. That is, nobody was complaining about the walk. Mick and Ed were still arguing about the car going off the road.

Blood had soaked through my hat and then frozen.

"How close are we?" I asked.

"I don't know," said Mr. Martin.

To be very clear, I was not bluffing. If Mr. Martin failed to bring me to Todd's resting place, I was going to take whatever measures were necessary to set him on the right path.

We kept walking. My pants were soaked all the way through, and I was surprised I could hold on to the flashlight and shovel, since I could barely feel anything below my elbow.

At least we had our trail in the snow to guide us back to civilization. We wouldn't all get lost out here and freeze to death.

That was about the only positive aspect of this I could think of right now. I'd known this was going to be hell on earth—well, frozen-over hell on earth—but it was worse than I'd expected. I wanted to move somewhere warm when this was over.

"I think that's the spot," said Mr. Martin, pointing ahead.

"Are you sure?" I asked.

"No, I'm not sure. How many fucking times do I have to say it? I *think* it *might* be the spot. Shine your flashlight on that tree. That one. No, to the right. Yes, this could be it. No promises."

It was going to take forever to dig through this frozen ground. I wanted to make sure that Mr. Martin wasn't just choosing a place to shut us up and buy himself some time.

"If you're wrong, we're going to place your hand flat against a tree," I said. "Then I'm going to let Ed smash it with a shovel as hard as he possibly can."

"I'm surprised we're not best friends, considering how sadistic you are," said Mr. Martin.

"Is that where you want us to dig?"

"Yes."

"Okay. Thank you. How far down is he?"

"A couple of feet."

"We're going to work in quick shifts," I announced. "Ed, Mick, and I will start. Then we'll switch to Tina, Burt, and Josh." I'd considered giving Tina an exemption from the digging part, but I decided it might offend her. "If you're not digging, you're responsible for holding the flashlights, and for beating the shit out of Mr. Martin if he tries to escape."

Josh gave me his snow shovel and the digging began. I had the best tool for the job, but Ed and Mick were keeping pace using the wrong kinds of shovels.

It wasn't long before we'd cleared out the snow.

Burt unscrewed the cap on his gasoline can and poured the

fluid all over the cleared-out area. I had no idea how well this was going to work, but it couldn't hurt, unless somebody got caught in the burst of flame and set their clothes and hair on fire. We'd be careful.

When the gasoline can was empty, we all stepped way back. Burt lit a match and tossed it onto the burial site.

There was a huge *whoosh* as the gasoline ignited. The heat from the fire felt wonderful, but it disappeared all too quickly.

"That didn't do shit," said Mr. Martin.

We returned to the area and began to dig.

22

M
r. Martin was right. The gasoline hadn't done any good, at least as far as I could tell. A pickaxe would've been much more helpful, but none of us owned one. We weren't really digging with our shovels; it was more like we were chipping away at the frozen ground.

We handed the shovels over to Tina, Burt, and Josh and gave them their turn.

After a few minutes, we switched back. We were making very slow progress, but we were still making progress. I'd stay out here all night if I had to. And if we dug down a couple of feet and found nothing, I might splatter Mr. Martin's hand myself.

We were digging a rectangle about the size of a coffin, even though Todd wouldn't be in a coffin.

The process got easier as we went along. Not that the ground was less frozen a foot down, but we were finding a rhythm. When I broke off a particularly large chunk of the dirt, I actually smiled at my accomplishment, before remembering the grim nature of the task.

Nobody gave up.

Mr. Martin looked angry and jittery. He didn't make any attempt to escape—he simply watched us work in silence.

We'd dug about two feet down.

Another large chunk of dirt came loose, revealing something black.

"Let me have your flashlight," I told Tina. She handed it to me and I crouched down to get a closer look. It was part of a garbage bag.

I tore it away. Underneath it was the sole of a shoe.

I thought I'd been digging at the front of the grave, by Todd's head. If this was the sole of his shoe, then we were an entire body-length off, and all of the other digging had been a waste. But there was a shoe in the ground. Though I obviously couldn't identify Todd's shoe by the rubber sole, it suddenly seemed very likely that Mr. Martin had indeed taken us to the correct spot.

"We're only going to dig here," I said, pointing to a spot in the center. We didn't need to dig him all the way up. The state troopers could do that. I just needed to know that it was him.

I didn't want to accidentally jam the shovel blade into his face, so I wanted to expose his chest, see what the buried body was wearing.

I did it myself, moving with renewed vigor. I refused to let anybody take over. I dug down until I reached the garbage bag, and then tore it open, revealing light green fabric.

Todd had been wearing a light green shirt when he was abducted.

The realization hit me so hard that I collapsed. Todd was dead. I'd known this. I'd suspected it in the days after his disappearance, and known it after the time that I pretended to interview Mr. Martin before pulling a gun on him. Todd was not living happily in California with a foster family. He was not chained in a basement, praying for rescue. He was dead in the frozen ground beneath me.

I sobbed. Nobody said anything, giving me the moment I needed, until Tina finally put her hand on my shoulder.

"We should go," she said.

I wiped my nose on the back of my glove and nodded. I stood up.

Mr. Martin was staring at me. He looked amused.

"Burn in hell," I told him.

"You won," he said. "How do you feel?"

"Don't talk to him," said Tina. "He's going to prison for the rest of his life. He doesn't have any more power over you."

"Look, I know it's cold as crap out here," said Ed, "but we don't all have to go back. A couple of us could stay here and watch over this asshole, and the rest of you can go get help."

"That's a good idea," I said. "I'll stay."

"Can we trust you not to bash his head in with a shovel?"

"Yeah. I need him alive."

"Okay."

"I'll stay," said Tina.

"You sure?" Ed asked. "You look like you're freezing to death."

"We're all freezing to death."

"That's true. You two better not get it on while we're gone. Although I guess that would be a good way to generate warmth. I take that back. You two better get it on while we're gone." Ed grinned, but nobody else seemed amused. We'd succeeded, but it was difficult to be in a celebratory mood standing next to where my friend was buried.

"I asked you a question," Mr. Martin said to me.

"And I told you to burn in hell."

"You won. How do you feel?"

"I feel fucking amazing."

"So, Curtis, I'm going to share a fact about my personal life with you, and I'm going to let you take as long as you need for it to sink in. This fact won't mean anything to your friends. I'm directing it right at you. Are you ready?"

"Sure."

"Both of my parents are dead."

"Okay. So?"

"Like I said. Take as long as you need."

I had no idea what the hell he was talking about. Was he trying to play mind games with me? If he thought he could get out of this by messing with my head, he was sorely—

Then I understood. Right before hanging up the phone, he'd said "*Tell Mom I love her.*"

"I see from your face that you figured it out. Do you want to share it with the others?"

"He was on the phone when I went into the basement," I said. "He said to tell his mom that he loved her, then he hung up."

"And you assumed that I was talking to a relative. A brother. A sister. An aunt or uncle. Any of those. That's what you assumed, right?"

"Right."

"So, Curtis, have you known me to bluff?"

"No."

"Correct. When I told you that I had a very dangerous friend, that turned out to be absolutely true, right? I wasn't making him up, was I? He paid you a scary little visit."

"Yes." I'm sure I was imagining it, but it felt like the wound on my head was suddenly leaking fresh, warm blood.

"Good. We're on the same page. So when I tell you that 'Tell Mom I love her' was a code phrase, do you think I'm pulling your leg? Or do you think my buddy went straight into action? We've been out here for a long time. Hours. Plenty of time for my pal to go get your mommy and daddy and bring them to a secret spot."

"You're lying," I said.

"Didn't we just establish that I don't bluff? You're more than welcome to believe that I'm lying. You can hurry back to the car, and stop at the first house you find. Borrow their phone. Call home. Nobody will answer."

I believed him. I fucking believed him.

I picked up the shovel. "Take me to them or I'll break your neck."

"You don't have to threaten me. I was going to take you to them anyway." Mr. Martin pointed to Tina. "You get to come with us, too. I feel like you two may be lovebirds. The rest of you aren't going anywhere. I can't force you to stay right here by the corpse, but I can say that if I see you following us, your friend's parents will be skinned alive. Tell them I'm serious, Curtis."

"He's serious," I said.

"You can keep the shovels, but hand over the flashlights. All of them. Give them to the girl."

"No way," said Ed. "Screw that."

"Curtis just got finished telling you that I'm serious. I mean, he literally just finished saying that. Let me explain this clearly, okay? You lose. You. Have. Lost. Your friend was in a no-win situation as soon as I hung up that phone. So give the girl your flashlights. I'm not trying to make you freeze to death out here. I'm just slowing you down. And somebody untie my fucking hands, okay?"

While I cut the rope binding Mr. Martin's hands, the others reluctantly handed their flashlights to Tina. She shoved them into the pockets of her jacket.

"Let her stay," I said.

Mr. Martin shook his head. "No."

"C'mon. She's not part of this."

"Of course she's part of this. We just dug up your dead friend."

"I will cooperate with whatever you want if you let her stay here."

"You will cooperate with whatever I want either way. You have no power right now, Curtis. None. Zero. When you argue with me like this, all you're doing is making me a little bit angrier, and trust me, I'm a bubbling fucking cauldron of rage."

"Let's just go," said Tina. "We don't want anything to happen to your parents."

"See?" said Mr. Martin. "She's way more practical than you are."

"Leave us one flashlight," said Ed.

"No. And if you ask me again, I'll take your jackets, too." He gestured to Mick. "Oh, hey, I almost forgot. Give me my car keys."

Mick, giving him a look of raw hatred, took the keys out of his pocket and handed them over.

"Let's go," said Mr. Martin. "I'd better not see the rest of you in the rearview mirror."

We left, abandoning the people who'd risked their lives to help me.

Since we could follow the trail we made on the way there, the way back went significantly faster. I tried not to think about Mom and Dad, but blood-soaked images kept flashing through my mind.

What if it was already too late? What if Mr. Martin had been bluffing, but the bluff was him saying that my parents were still alive. His friend might have slashed their throats while they slept.

We walked in silence. I wanted to apologize to Tina. And I wanted to reassure her that everything would be all right, but I didn't want to lie to her, and I didn't want to give Mr. Martin something to ridicule. I'd save the apology for when this was over. I'd make it up to her.

The car was still there, which honestly surprised me a bit

because with the way things were going I'd kind of expected it to be stolen or vandalized.

"You're driving," Mr. Martin said to me.

"I can't drive."

"You're old enough for a learner's permit, at least."

"Yeah, but I don't have one."

"That's insane. What kind of kid doesn't get their learner's permit on their fourteenth birthday?"

"The kind whose best friend had just disappeared."

"Okay, okay, fair enough." He looked over at Tina. "What about you?"

"I don't turn fourteen until next month."

"Well, fuck. I guess it doesn't matter if I drive. You try anything, and I mean *anything*, and we won't make it to our destination. And if I don't show up, my friend gets to do whatever he wants to Mommy and Daddy. I know the kind of things he'll do if I'm right there watching. I can't even *imagine* what he'll do if he has privacy."

We got in the car. I took the front seat and Tina sat in the back. Mr. Martin turned on the engine and we sat there for a few minutes, waiting for it to warm up. Then he turned the car around and we drove back to Chena Hot Springs Road.

"It's not all that far," said Mr. Martin, making a left turn when we reached the paved road, which would take us further away from Fairbanks. "You'll be reunited with them pretty soon."

I said nothing.

Mr. Martin chuckled. "Ah, the optimism of youth. I wish I were young again."

"What are you talking about?"

"You think you can still get out of this. I would be wallowing in nihilism and despair. But you, you actually believe that you're going to save your parents and have a happy ending with your girlfriend back there. It's cute. *Delusional,* but cute. I like it. Looking forward to extinguishing it."

A few miles later, he turned onto a plowed road without a street sign.

After a long and winding path, he pulled up in front of a small log cabin. Smoke billowed from a chimney. Another car was parked in front of it. Mr. Martin shut off the engine.

"Here we are," he said.

I opened my door.

"Wait, hold on," said Mr. Martin. "Not yet. Have either of you ever visited a prison? I don't mean to visit a family member who held up a convenience store or something, I mean actually toured the inside of a prison."

"No," I said.

"You?" he asked Tina.

"No."

"Well, what happens is that they have this rule that if somehow you are unlucky enough to be taken hostage, they will not release the prisoner. The prisoner can have a sharpened spoon to your throat and threaten to spray your blood all over Cell Block B, and they aren't going to open that door. It seems cold-hearted, but it makes perfect sense. You don't want prisoners thinking they can escape by taking hostages. The official policy of the United States of America is that we don't negotiate with terrorists. Oh, we'll talk to them, but we won't give them anything in exchange for releasing hostages from a hijacked plane. Again, if terrorists know that we will not cave in to their demands, no matter what, they won't bother trying. Do you get the point I'm trying to make here, Curtis?"

"Don't try to take you hostage?"

"Exactly! Smart kid. My buddy will not release your parents in exchange for my life. If you try it, he'll just laugh at you. I'm glad I didn't have to explain that to you."

"Can I get out of the car now?" I asked.

"In a second. My friend's name is Griffin."

"Okay."

"Kind of weird that I told you that, huh? It gives you extra information in case you try to snitch on us. It's almost like, if you really try to read into it, I'm not worried about you knowing things that you could use against us. Hmmm. Do you get *that* point, Curtis?"

"Yes."

"The optimism of youth again. I've basically told you that you will not be coming out of that log cabin. And yet you're still going to come with me to try to save your parents, aren't you? Of course you are. Again, I wish I could find my own inner delusional child."

Part of me—a very small part—did think that I should throw open the door, shout "*Run!*" and see if Tina and I could successfully flee. Mr. Martin didn't seem particularly worried about that outcome. Maybe that's what he wanted—a chance to chase us through the woods. To hunt us.

Or maybe he thought I wouldn't leave my parents to die a horrible death.

If so, he was absolutely correct.

We all got out of the car.

"How do I know they're in there?" I asked.

"I could bring out a head or two, if you want."

"I mean it. I know you say that you never bluff, but for all I know they're perfectly safe at home. I'm not going to be stupid enough to just walk into a trap."

"I hear you," said Mr. Martin. He walked over to the front door, knocked twice, then opened it. "Hey, Griffin, it's me! Yeah, I've got him. Plus a bonus. But he wants proof."

Mr. Martin turned back to face me. "You'd recognize your mother's scream, right?"

A piercing scream came from inside the house.

I'd never heard her scream in pain like that, but it was definitely Mom.

23

Tina and I followed Mr. Martin through the front door.

"Take off your jackets and stay a while," he said.

I shook my head. "We're fine."

"I said, take off your jackets. Boots too. You can leave on your hat so that we don't have to look at that gory wound on your head."

Tina and I took off our jackets and boots. Mr. Martin didn't offer to take them for us, so we set them on the floor. Inside, the cabin looked just like a regular house except for the log walls. It was nice and toasty warm. I wondered how Ed and the others were doing.

"I'd give you the grand tour, but I know who you're here to see. Let's go."

We followed Mr. Martin down a staircase into the basement.

There was a roaring fire going in a small fireplace. That was the only pleasant sight in the basement.

Griffin was down there. It was indeed the same guy who'd broken into my house and threatened me. Not that I'd doubted it would be, but it wouldn't have surprised me to find out that Mr. Martin's social circle included more than one other killer.

There were two beds, side by side. Mom was chained to one and Dad was chained to the other. It wasn't just handcuffs—these were thick chains with actual shackles around their wrists and ankles. Mom was in a bloodstained yellow nightgown and Dad was in bloodstained blue pajamas. They both had a couple of cuts on their faces.

Griffin was wrapping duct tape around Mom's head. Apparently he'd torn it off so she could scream.

"Damn, Griffin, it looks like you've already gotten started."

Griffin smiled and shrugged. "Took you a while to get here."

"Oh, yeah. It went to complete shit. I can't go back to my house ever again."

"Well, you're welcome here as long as you want."

"Thanks."

"And you were looking to get out anyway."

"Yeah, but still." Mr. Martin pointed at Tina. "Hey, lock her up for me, will you?"

"We only have two beds."

"So handcuff her to the radiator."

"All right." Griffin picked up a gun. "Hey, girlie, come on over here."

Tina didn't move.

"Can I shoot her if she disobeys a direct order?" Griffin asked.

"Sure," said Mr. Martin.

"Hey, girlie, come on over here before I shoot you in the stomach."

Tina glanced over at me. What was I supposed to tell her? Not to do what he said? It was killing me to feel this helpless, but there had to be a solution. There had to be a way to convince Mr. Martin that he could let us all go and we'd stay silent about it forever.

I gave Tina a small nod.

She walked over to Griffin. He searched around for a moment, found a pair of handcuffs on a shelf, and snapped one of the bracelets around her wrist.

She lashed at him with her free hand, as if trying to rake her fingernails across his eyes.

Griffin punched her in the face. Blood sprayed from Tina's nose as she dropped to the floor.

"Wow, she's a vicious one," said Griffin. He laughed.

Mr. Martin didn't laugh. "Can you just lock her up, please?"

"Sure, sure." Griffin dragged Tina, who wasn't unconscious but was barely moving, over to the radiator. He snapped the free bracelet around the metal. "Why are you such a sourpuss?" he asked Mr. Martin. "Maybe you should sit by the fireplace for a few minutes and warm yourself up."

"Nah, I'm fine." Mr. Martin looked over at me. "So, Curtis, are you starting to realize just how badly you messed up?"

"Yeah," I said. There had to be a way out of this. Sure, my parents were chained to beds, my girlfriend was handcuffed to a radiator, I had no weapons, and I was up against a pair of adult psychopaths, but I could save the day, right? No problem. Barely a challenge.

"How do you want to do this?" Mr. Martin asked. "Do you want to choose which one of your parents dies first? Do you want us to pin your eyes open so you have to watch every cut? Do you want to sacrifice yourself for them?"

"Let me do it," I said.

"Excuse me?"

"Let me do it. They didn't believe me when I told them about you. When I got arrested, they left me in jail overnight to teach me a lesson."

"Oh, that's cold," said Griffin. "Sounds like my mom and dad."

"They were going to send me away to boarding school. So why should I care if you kill them? If you let me do it, I can't go to the police. I'm just as guilty as you are. I'll walk out of here and you'll never see me again."

"What about your girlfriend?" Mr. Martin asked.

"You have to let her go, too."

"Why wouldn't she go to the police?"

"I'd make sure she didn't."

"You have that much control over her, huh?"

"I guarantee she won't say anything."

"What about your friends?"

"What about them?"

"You think they won't squeal?"

"I wasn't saying that you could return to your normal life," I explained. "I'm saying that since you'd already planned to leave town, if you let me kill my mom and dad, we could go our separate ways."

"That's an interesting plan," said Mr. Martin. "If I thought I could trust you, I'd consider it. But you haven't proven yourself to be very trustworthy, have you? Anyway, Griffin was looking forward to torturing and killing your parents. I wouldn't want to rob him of that experience."

"I wouldn't mind watching the kid have a go at it," said Griffin.

"Seriously?" Mr. Martin asked.

"Sure, why not? There's an axe on the shelf. Let him chop off an arm. I'll shoot him if he gets out of line."

"Is that what you want?" Mr. Martin asked me. "Do you want to chop off your mother's arm?"

"I'd rather shatter my dad's kneecap," I said. "He broke his knee before and said it was the worst pain he'd ever felt in his entire life."

This was a lie. My dad, to the best of my knowledge, had never had a serious knee injury. But I hoped it sounded credible.

I didn't want them to give me an axe. I was eyeing something else.

"Damn, this kid's a little sociopath," said Griffin.

"Maybe."

"Let him try. See if he'll actually splinter his dad's knee."

I purposely didn't look at Mom or Dad's faces. I didn't want to be permanently haunted by their reactions.

"All right," said Mr. Martin. "Do you have a hammer?"

"On the shelf."

"What about the fireplace poker?" I asked.

"Sure," said Griffin. "You can break some bones with that. Or you could hold it in the flames for a few minutes. Press it against their bare skin."

"I don't want to brand him. I want to break his knee."

Griffin walked over to the fireplace and picked up the poker. "Remember that I've got a gun," he said. "You try anything funny, and I'll shoot your tiny dick off."

"I understand."

He handed me the poker, then walked over to Dad's bed, standing near his head.

I walked over to the bed as well. I tapped the poker into my palm a few times, as if testing the weight.

I couldn't fake the hit. I had to hit him as hard as I could. This was going to be awful.

I hoisted the fireplace poker over my head, then slammed it down on Dad's upper left leg. His shriek of pain was muffled by the duct tape but still agonizing to hear. I'm pretty sure I'd heard a crunch.

"Oh, shit!" said Griffin. "He's not playing around!"

"Missed his knee, though," said Mr. Martin.

I raised the poker again. I didn't want to shatter Dad's kneecap. He might never fully recover from that.

I slammed it down in the same spot. Something else cracked. His shriek was even worse this time.

"I felt that one in my *own* knee," said Griffin. "That's brutal. If I ever have kids, I'm never going to leave them in jail overnight. It turns them into lunatics."

I wasn't quite getting the reaction I wanted. Griffin was still pointing the gun at me.

I needed to take it up another level.

This time, instead of holding the poker like a golf club, I held it pointing straight down above his leg. The sharp point of the poker was aimed at the spot where I'd already broken bones.

I couldn't understand what Dad said to me through the duct tape, but he seemed to be begging me not to do this.

I looked over at Griffin, winked, and slammed it down. A bit of blood sprayed as the iron point went deep into his leg.

More shrieking.

Griffin's mouth was wide open with delight. He was *loving* this. He couldn't believe what he was seeing.

He'd finally lowered the gun.

I pulled the tip of the poker out of Dad's leg and wound it back for a swing as I strode toward Griffin. He was only two steps away.

He raised the gun again.

I swung the poker as hard as I could.

I got him right in the side of the chin. Some blood and several teeth sprayed into the air, and suddenly his jaw was no longer even with the top half of his face.

He howled and dropped the gun.

His screams, not muffled by duct tape, were far worse than Dad's. He staggered around, clutching his mutilated face. A large piece of his tongue slipped out of his mouth and fell to the floor— apparently he'd bitten it off.

I turned my attention to Mr. Martin.

He'd picked up the axe.

He quickly moved over to Mom's bed, and held the blade over her neck.

"Put down the poker," he told me. "Right now. Put it down or I'll chop her head off." It was hard to hear him over Griffin's wailing, but I got the idea. Mom struggled against the chains, though of course that did no good.

I dropped the poker.

"Kick it out of the way. I mean kick it hard. I want to hear some toes break."

I kicked the poker away. It didn't go very far.

"Put the axe down," I told him.

"Down where? Down into her neck. Sure, I can do that."

"Drop it on the floor."

"Oh, wait, you think this is a negotiation," said Mr. Martin. "No, no, that's not what's happening here. I gave you an order and you followed it. But you don't get to tell me what to do in return. The only good thing for you is that you won't have to see what Griffin would've done with your mom's severed head."

He raised the axe.

Griffin was still staggering around, holding his jaw as if trying to keep it from completely detaching from his face.

He walked past Tina.

She stuck out her leg and tripped him.

Griffin fell to the floor, landing face-first.

It is not possible, using mere words, to successfully convey the scope of Griffin's reaction to his already broken jaw smashing into the concrete floor. It simply cannot be done. The noise he made was almost beyond the ability of humankind to comprehend. I do not believe it could ever be duplicated.

There was no way for Mr. Martin to *not* look over at his friend.

I had to make a decision in an instant. If I charged at Mr.

Martin, would he swing the axe down, chopping off my mother's head, or would he use that axe to defend himself against my attack?

What would he do?

I thought, in that instant, that he would use the axe for self-preservation.

I had to move fast. I had to move really, really fast. I couldn't be Curtis Black, the overweight and clumsy fourteen-year-old. I had to be Curtis Black, Olympic athlete, moving with lightning speed.

I ran at him.

My feet did not slip out from under me.

I didn't accidentally bash into Dad's bed.

I didn't trip on the fireplace poker.

I charged at Mr. Martin, and I'd guessed correctly. He did not slam the blade down onto Mom's neck. Instead, he adjusted his grip on it, so that he could slam it into my chest.

I got there first. When absolutely, positively necessary, this fat kid could *move*.

He was expecting me to try to wrench the axe away from him. That made sense. It would've been a solid strategy. In fact, it was probably less risky that what I did try to do, which was punch him in the throat.

It was a great fucking punch.

Mr. Martin's eyes went wide and he let out a gasp.

The axe slipped out of his hands.

On the way down, it lopped off his ear. Then it bounced off his shoulder and fell to the floor.

Mr. Martin just kind of stood there for a moment, trying to breathe, not seeming entirely aware that there was blood spurting from the side of his head.

I punched him in the stomach. He doubled over, vomited, and then stood back up.

So I punched him again.

He stumbled backwards and smacked into the wall. Then he slid to the floor.

I picked up the axe.

"Curtis, don't!" Tina shouted.

"I'm not going to kill him," I said. That would make things a lot harder for me when I tried to get this whole mess straightened out.

I was going to beat him unconscious with the wooden axe handle. But I wondered if I might cause brain damage. I didn't want that.

Mr. Martin closed his eyes and slumped over to the side.

And with that, I'd won.

24

A lot happened after that.

I hurried upstairs and found a phone. I called 911. I didn't know the exact location of the log cabin, but I was able to give them enough information to find it.

I went back downstairs and got the duct tape off Mom and Dad. My emotions went absolutely berserk as I sobbed and apologized and swore that I had no other choice. I couldn't think of any other way to save them.

I couldn't find a key to Tina's handcuffs or to Mom and Dad's chains, so we had to wait for the state troopers to arrive before they could get free. It was a long wait. It felt like it took forever for Griffin to finally lose consciousness and shut the hell up.

But as you might have guessed, the events of the first night of winter in Fairbanks, Alaska in 1979 made it a lot easier to plead the case that those two ounces of marijuana in my backpack weren't mine.

Todd's parents came back to Alaska to have a proper funeral for their son.

The bodies of the other children were found, giving their families some measure of resolution and peace.

There was kind of a weird parent/child dynamic for a while after that. On one hand, I'd rescued my parents from a nightmarish fate. On the other hand, I was kind of responsible for them being kidnapped. But they hadn't believed me when I told them that Mr. Martin had framed me. And even though I was technically their savior, I had broken my dad's leg and stabbed him with a fireplace poker. So things were...weird. Very, very weird.

Ed, Mick, Burt, and Josh did not freeze to death. I was happy about that. They all basked in the brief glory of being the heroes who'd discovered Todd's body. We didn't become friends, though. Our personalities and interests were just too different.

Tina's dad withdrew the threat to kill me if I saw his daughter.

Backtracking a bit, I'm not suggesting that Tina and I had started making out in the basement while we waited for help to arrive. That would be depraved. I'm also not suggesting that as we walked out to the waiting ambulance, I took her in my arms and kissed her under the beauty of the Northern Lights.

No, like my relationship with my parents, it was weird for a while.

But we got over it.

I was un-expelled from school, and finished up the year with a solid B-minus average. It could've been a B, but when Tina and I got together to study, we often failed to study.

That summer, in a highly publicized trial, Mr. Gerald Martin was found guilty on all counts and sentenced to life in prison. Griffin had been carried out of the log cabin in a coma and never woke up, so he had no trial.

Tina and I dated all through high school. Our senior prom picture is embarrassingly bad.

We dated all through college. She graduated with honors. I did not.

We got married in 1989. Our son Matt was born in 1990. It seemed kind of close, but if you did the math, he was born nine and a half months after our wedding.

Our daughter Vivian was born in 1993, the same year that Mr. Martin died in prison. He wasn't beaten to death by his fellow prisoners, unfortunately, nor was it something slow and painful. Cardiac arrest. His heart basically said "Fuck this guy" and gave out. I honestly wasn't sure how to feel about this, so I decided to play with my kids instead.

We made it through Y2K without the world ending.

Our second daughter Marcie was born in 2003. You may be thinking that ten years is a pretty long gap between a second and third child, and wondering if we planned it this way. The answer is, no, we did not. In fact, we said "What the hell?" a lot. But she turned out to be a happy accident and we love her even more than her brother and sister. (I'm just kidding. Hi, Matt! Hi, Vivian! I'm sorry you had to read about your mom telling me I could touch her boob! And also that one part where your grandparents had makeup sex. I didn't like writing about it any more than you liked reading about it.)

In 2012, the grandkids started popping out at the rate of one a year for the next five years. This was very odd because Tina and I were *clearly* too young to have grandchildren. Sure, we were getting unnervingly close to fifty, but still, we *felt* young, and that should've counted for something.

In 2019, Tina's father died. Unlike Mr. Martin's death, his was slow and awful, but he got to meet all five of his great-grandchildren.

As I write this in 2020, both of my parents are alive and well. In case you were wondering, yes, Dad's leg healed fine, but yes, he has a scar from where I stabbed him with the poker. He shows it to me often. I wish he'd stop. Seriously.

Overall, we're doing well. There have been plenty of challenges along the way, yet compared to a five-month standoff against a serial killer, they haven't been so bad.

I know I've spent a lot of time talking about abductions and psychopaths and broken jaws and stuff, but ultimately I consider this to be the story of how Tina and I fell in love. Though you may not have got that impression while you were reading it, you're not the one trying to get lucky after typing "The End," so you can take from this story whatever you wish.

I love you, Sweetie.

— The End —

ACKNOWLEDGMENTS

Thank you to Jamie La Chance, Tod Clark, Donna Fitzpatrick, Paul Goblirsch, Darrell Z. Grizzle, Kate Halpern, Lynne Hansen, Jim Morey, and Paul Synuria II for their help with this novel.

BOOKS BY JEFF STRAND

The Odds - When invited to a game that offers a 99% chance of winning fifty thousand dollars, Ethan rejoices at the chance to recoup his gambling losses. But as the game continues, the odds constantly change, and the risks become progressively deadlier...

Allison. She can break your bones using her mind. And she's trying very hard not to hurt you.

Wolf Hunt 3. George, Lou, Ally, and Eugene are back in another werewolf-laden adventure.

Clowns Vs. Spiders. Choose your side!

My Pretties. A serial kidnapper may have met his match in the two young ladies who walk the city streets at night, using themselves as bait...

Five Novellas. A compilation of *Stalking You Now, An Apocalypse of Our Own, Faint of Heart, Kutter,* and *Facial*.

Ferocious. The creatures of the forest are dead...and hungry!

Bring Her Back. A tale of revenge and madness.

Sick House. A home invasion from beyond the grave.

Bang Up. A filthy comedic thriller. "You want to pay me to sleep with your wife?" is just the start of the story.

Cold Dead Hands. Ten people are trapped in a freezer during a terrorist attack on a grocery store.

How You Ruined My Life (Young Adult). Sixteen-year-old Rod has a pretty cool life until his cousin Blake moves in and slowly destroys everything he holds dear.

Everything Has Teeth. A third collection of short tales of horror and macabre comedy.

An Apocalypse of Our Own. Can the Friend Zone survive the end of the world?

Stranger Things Have Happened (Young Adult). Teenager Marcus Millian III is determined to be one of the greatest magicians who ever lived. Can he make a live shark disappear from a tank?

Cyclops Road. When newly widowed Evan Portin gives a woman named Harriett a ride out of town, she says she's on a cross-country journey to slay a Cyclops. Is she crazy, or...?

Blister. While on vacation, cartoonist Jason Tray meets the town legend, a hideously disfigured woman who lives in a shed.

The Greatest Zombie Movie Ever (Young Adult). Three best friends with more passion than talent try to make the ultimate zombie epic.

Kumquat. A road trip comedy about TV, hot dogs, death, and obscure fruit.

I Have a Bad Feeling About This (Young Adult). Geeky, non-athletic Henry Lambert is sent to survival camp, which is bad enough *before* the trio of murderous thugs show up.

Pressure. What if your best friend was a killer...and he wanted you to be just like him? Bram Stoker Award nominee for Best Novel.

Dweller. The lifetime story of a boy and his monster. Bram Stoker Award nominee for Best Novel.

A Bad Day For Voodoo. A young adult horror/comedy about why sticking pins in a voodoo doll of your history teacher isn't always the best idea. Bram Stoker Award nominee for Best Young Adult Novel.

Dead Clown Barbecue. A collection of demented stories about severed noses, ventriloquist dummies, giant-sized vampires, sibling stabbings, and lots of other messed-up stuff.

Dead Clown Barbecue Expansion Pack. A few more stories for those who couldn't get enough.

Wolf Hunt. Two thugs for hire. One beautiful woman. And one vicious frickin' werewolf.

Wolf Hunt 2. New wolf. Same George and Lou.

The Sinister Mr. Corpse. The feel-good zombie novel of the year.

Benjamin's Parasite. A rather disgusting action/horror/comedy about why getting infected with a ghastly parasite is unpleasant.

Fangboy. A dark and demented fairy tale for adults.

Facial. Greg has just killed the man he hired to kill one of his wife's many lovers. Greg's brother desperately needs a dead body. It's kind of related to the lion corpse that he found in his basement. This is the normal part of the story.

Kutter. A serial killer finds a Boston terrier, and it might just make him into a better person.

Faint of Heart. To get her kidnapped husband back, Melody has to relive her husband's nightmarish weekend, step-by-step...and survive.

Mandibles. Giant killer ants wreaking havoc in the big city!

Stalking You Now. A twisty-turny thriller soon to be the feature film *Mindy Has To Die.*

Graverobbers Wanted (No Experience Necessary). First in the Andrew Mayhem series.

Single White Psychopath Seeks Same. Second in the Andrew Mayhem series.

Casket For Sale (Only Used Once). Third in the Andrew Mayhem series.

Lost Homicidal Maniac (Answers to "Shirley"). Fourth in the Andrew Mayhem series.

Cemetery Closing (Everything Must Go). Fifth in the Andrew Mayhem series.

Suckers (with JA Konrath). Andrew Mayhem meets Harry McGlade. Which one will prove to be more incompetent?

Gleefully Macabre Tales. A collection of thirty-two demented tales. Bram Stoker Award nominee for Best Collection.

Elrod McBugle on the Loose. A comedy for kids (and adults who were warped as kids).

The Haunted Forest Tour (with Jim Moore). The greatest theme park attraction in the world! Take a completely safe ride through an actual haunted forest! Just hope that your tram doesn't break down, because this forest is PACKED with monsters...

Draculas (with JA Konrath, Blake Crouch, and F. Paul Wilson). An outbreak of feral vampires in a secluded hospital. This one isn't much like *Twilight*.

For information on all of these books, visit Jeff Strand's more-or-less official website at http://www.JeffStrand.com

Subscribe to Jeff Strand's free monthly newsletter (which includes a brand-new original short story in every issue) at http://eepurl.com/bpv5br

And remember:

Readers who leave reviews deserve great big hugs!

Printed in Great Britain
by Amazon